Toni Donati—She's only three months old and already she needs a score card. She's been put in her father's care, who's temporarily left her with his brother Luc, who's recruited his secretary, Grace, who's pretending to be his fiancée, hoping to mollify the police, who've called the child welfare people, who believe that Grace and Luc are married.

Luc Salvatore—Simply put, he's every woman's dream. And he loves women—all women. Young and old, short and tall...well, you get the picture. He bowls them over like ninepins, including each and every secretary he's ever had. But his new secretary, Grace, isn't falling. Which intrigues him. *She* intrigues him.... And now that he needs Grace to pose as his fiancée so he can retain custody of his niece—maybe he'll discover why.

Grace Barnes—For a minister's daughter, this past year has been a revelation. Frankly, she didn't know she was capable of telling this many lies. Even her mousy appearance is a lie—all in an effort to resist Luc Salvatore's attractions. And you know what? *It isn't working!* Especially now that she's staying with him, pretending to be engaged.

Dear Reader,

Writing this book for Kids & Kisses brought to mind the first time I held my son. Seconds after he was born, the doctor rested him on my stomach. He lay facedown, sort of surprised by all the noise and confusion, amazed to discover he could fully stretch his little limbs and kick and squirm, delighted to discover he had a voice. I spoke to him... I can't remember what I said. I probably murmured his name—Matthew—and whispered those eternal words of love all mothers speak when they first lay eyes on their newborn child.

But what I remember most is his reaction to my voice. His little brow puckered and he tried to lift his head and peer into my face. He was the most beautiful creature I'd ever seen.

I fell in love in that instant. A lasting love. A forever love. My husband had given me this precious gift and it's been a gift that has only improved with age.

My husband's reaction when handed his newborn son? He turned white as a sheet and almost passed out. Fortunately a nurse snatched Matt away in the nick of time!

Children play such a big part when it comes to love and commitment and marriage. And in this story, one special little baby plays a vital role in sparking a romance. I hope you enjoy *Who's Holding the Baby?* It brought back a lot of fond memories.

Sincerely,

Day Leclaire

WHO'S HOLDING THE BABY?
Day Leclaire

Harlequin Books

TORONTO • NEW YORK • LONDON
AMSTERDAM • PARIS • SYDNEY • HAMBURG
STOCKHOLM • ATHENS • TOKYO • MILAN
MADRID • WARSAW • BUDAPEST • AUCKLAND

To Frank Matthew Smith...
my one and only.
All my love—Mom.

ISBN 0-373-03338-9

WHO'S HOLDING THE BABY?

PROLOGUE

The Great Lie
Day 1 . . . and the games begin . . .

GRACE BARNES STOOD IN front of the door that read *Luciano Salvatore, President,* and took a deep breath. She could do it. Sure she could. All she had to do was knock. The man on the other side of the door would say, "Come in." She'd open the door, step into the office and her deception would begin. After that, she only had to keep her job with this man for one year and she'd receive the financing necessary to start her own business. What could be easier?

She shoved her tinted glasses higher on the bridge of her nose, checked to be sure that not a single hair had escaped the prim knot at the nape of her neck and tugged at the mud brown skirt and sweater that threatened to engulf her. All right, she was ready. She lifted her fist to knock, but before she could, the door opened.

And that's when she saw him for the first time. In that instant, she realized how badly she'd misjudged Dom Salvatore and how foolish she'd been not to give him credit for knowing his son. He'd warned her. Oh, he'd definitely warned her. Every assistant Luc hired fell in love with him and ended up making a mess of the work situation. But she'd thought Dom had exaggerated. He hadn't.

Luc Salvatore was the most gorgeous man she'd ever set eyes on. High, aristocratic cheekbones and a square cleft chin complemented a striking masculine face. Thick, dark brown hair fell in careless waves across his forehead, emphasizing eyes that held her with almost hypnotic power. He filled the doorway, and unable to help herself, she took several hasty steps backward.

"Well, well..." he said, folding his arms across his broad chest and leaning against the jamb. "Who have we here?" Although he didn't have his father's Italian accent, there was a similar underlying lilt to his deep, husky voice that brought to mind exotic climes and sultry nights.

"I'm... I'm Grace Barnes," she said. To her horror, she sounded almost timorous. This would never do! What was wrong with her?

Slowly he straightened and walked toward her. She stood rigidly, not daring to speak, not daring to so much as move. For some inexplicable reason her heart pounded and it became a struggle to draw breath. *Think of Baby Dream Toys,* she told herself. *Think of Mom planning for the day we'd open our own business.*

Utilizing every ounce of control she possessed, she held out a hand. "I'm Grace Barnes," she repeated in a cool, strong voice. "Your father hired me as your new assistant." To her relief, her fingers were rock steady.

He took her hand and shook it. "It's a pleasure to meet you, Miss Barnes. Or is it Mrs.?" He released her right hand and lifted her left, studying the glittering diamond decorating her finger. "Miss Barnes. Spoken for, but not yet taken. Our loss is..." he tilted his head to one side and lifted an eyebrow "... whose gain?"

She froze, staring up at him, staring into eyes that made her think of hot, liquid gold. She prayed her tinted lenses concealed her panic. She hadn't anticipated the question and she should have. "Will...William," she replied, picking the first name to pop into her head.

His mouth curved, his expression wickedly amused. "Our loss is Will-William's gain. Come on into my office. Let's get acquainted. Would you care for a drink? Coffee, tea? I even have freshly squeezed orange juice."

She followed him, trying to gather her composure. "Nothing, thank you," she said, once again affecting a calm, collected guise.

"Sit down. I assume my father told you I was out of the country during the interview process. Explain why he chose you from all the other applicants."

She didn't dare tell him the truth. Dom had specifically asked that she not mention they'd met through Salvatore's annual young-entrepreneur contest, a contest designed to help young businesspeople start their own companies. She'd hoped to win first prize—a monetary award that would have enabled her to open Baby Dream Toys. Unfortunately, she'd placed third, a mixed blessing. Though that prize wasn't sufficient to enable Grace to open her shop, it had, fortuitously, brought her to Dom's attention and given her the opportunity to fulfill her dream...if in a rather roundabout manner.

"I gather from what your father said that you've had trouble keeping your assistants," she finally replied. Which kept Dom from fully retiring, a situation he was desperate to correct. "He felt that wouldn't be a problem with me."

Luc's eyes narrowed. "Really? And why is that?"

"Because I'm serious about my work."

And because all she needed to do was keep her job as Luc's assistant for one year—and unlike his previous assistants, maintain a strictly professional relationship—

and she'd be given the financing to start her own business. There wasn't a chance she'd fall for Luc's charms and sacrifice her dream. Not a chance.

Luc inclined his head. "Let's hope so." He leaned back in his chair. "Tell me more about yourself."

Hesitantly, she complied, outlining the résumé that rested on his desk. And all the time she spoke he watched her. He watched the way she talked and the movement of her hands as she made a point. He scanned her tightly controlled hair and her face, virtually obliterated by the huge tinted lenses. Even the prim manner in which she sat—straight-backed, ankles crossed—didn't escape his attention.

She wondered if he saw through her disguise, realized her blond hair had been tinted drab brown with a temporary rinse, that she'd dressed in oversize, unattractive clothes, that her tinted glasses had nonprescription lenses. And what about the engagement ring? It rode her finger, an unfamiliar weight as well as an uncomfortable fabrication. She stirred uneasily. For a minister's daughter, duplicity came hard.

But she wanted to attain her dream. She wanted it more than anything in the world. And this temporary deception would get it for her.

"So," she concluded her recital, "I worked there for one year before being offered this job." With nothing left to say, she fell silent.

He didn't comment, simply completed his perusal, his odd golden eyes narrowed in thought, as though analyzing something that didn't quite add up. Grace sat perfectly still, realizing that this was it—lose her cool now and she'd blow the chance of a lifetime. She regarded him steadily, knowing that if she were to be successful working for this man, she'd need to maintain a very careful facade.

At long last he nodded. "Welcome aboard, Miss Barnes. As usual, Dad has shown excellent judgment. Let me show you to your desk." He stood and led the way into the outer office. "Here's your new home. Have a seat."

He held her chair out for her with such a natural, unconscious ease that she knew it must come from long ingrained habit. "Thank you," she murmured.

"Get familiar with the setting, take some time to explore the office area, have a cup of coffee or tea and report to me in an hour. Then we'll go over office procedure, and I'll explain how we do things around here and run through your duties. Though in all honesty there's only one thing I expect you to do."

She eyed him warily. "Which is?"

He grinned. "Whatever I say."

She stared at him uncertainly. He was a difficult man to nail down. Serious one minute, teasing the next. Add to that looks and intelligence and one final trait that would be the most difficult to deal with—a wicked sense of humor—and she could understand why women fell like ninepins. Was it possible that his charm was an unconscious part of his personality, that he didn't even realize all those women had lost their hearts to him? Time would tell.

Meanwhile, she could think of only one way to deal with him. "'Whatever you say' isn't in my job description," she informed him in her most businesslike voice. "You'll have to be more specific than that, Mr. Salvatore."

His eyes glittered with laughter. "I'll see what I can do. Oh . . . And one more thing."

He circled her desk, standing directly behind her. She felt his hand brush her spine, following the row of buttons to the nape of her neck. It was as though she'd been touched with a live wire. She started out of her chair, but he pressed her gently back into her seat.

"Hold still, *cara mia*," he murmured. "Just for a moment."

With a final glancing touch, he released her. Crossing to the front of the desk, he looked down, a crooked smile curving his mouth. She gazed up at him, once again captured by those strange golden eyes.

"What were you doing?" she demanded.

"I was doing you a favor. Your button had come unfastened." His voice lowered confidingly. "And I thought you looked like the sort of woman who isn't comfortable unless she's all buttoned up." Without another word, he returned to his office and gently closed the door.

And that, she realized with a sudden flash of intuition, would set the pattern for their relationship. She'd play the role of the stoic professional, and he'd be unable to resist pricking her composure, teasing a less-than-professional response from her.

Releasing her breath in a long sigh, Grace stared at the calendar centered on the desk. One year stretched before her in a string of endless days. Three hundred and sixty-five days, to be precise. It seemed a lifetime. Without giving herself time to consider, she opened the desk drawer and shoved through the paraphernalia cluttered inside until she found a bright red marker. With great deliberation, and even greater satisfaction, she slashed an *X* through the first day of her year-long sentence.

And in that instant Grace realized just what she'd let herself in for... and just how long and difficult the next year would be.

CHAPTER ONE

The Great Lie
Day 337 and all is well until now...

"MORNING, MISS BARNES." The security guard greeted her with a cheerful grin. "Early to work, I see. Same as always, rain or shine."

Grace leaned her dripping umbrella against his desk and stripped off her gloves. "More rain than shine, I'm afraid," she observed, offering him a warm smile in return.

"It is blustery out there. Did you have a good weekend?"

"Splendid, thank you, Edward." She tucked her gloves into the pocket of her raincoat. "And you?"

"Drove to the mountains with the wife and kids. The forecast called for snow and they don't often get the chance to see it falling. All the Thanksgiving decorations were out." He shook his head. "It was quite a sight."

An onslaught of memories from past holiday celebrations with her family brought a wistful smile to Grace's lips. The house had always been filled with friends and family and with the odors of freshly baked pies and breads. Her father would build a huge, roaring fire and her mother would festoon the mantel with gourds and Indian corn and her pilgrim candlestick holders.

Tears pricked her eyes. Lord, how she missed all that. "The first snowfall of the season," she whispered longingly. "It must have been glorious."

"You and your fiancé ever do that? Drive to the mountains to see the snow?"

She shook her head, still lost in memories. "Never."

"Aw, that's a real shame."

His expression was pitying and right away she realized she'd made a mistake, forgotten for a split second the role she had to play. "I'll suggest a drive to the mountains for next weekend. I'm certain he'll think it's a terrific idea."

"Yeah, sure."

"Really. We'll go next weekend."

She knew the security guard didn't believe her. His brow creased and she could see him fishing around for something more to add, something that would help salvage her dignity. Which was a laugh. After almost a full year of this masquerade, she had very little dignity left to salvage.

"Your fiancé is a lucky man," he said at last, "having such an...an...*elegant* woman as yourself for his bride-to-be."

She smiled wryly. He seemed intent on painting himself further and further into his corner. Grace decided it was time to put the poor man out of his misery.

"My fiancé is a fine man," she lied smoothly. Practice certainly did make perfect. "I've never met anyone more eager to please. He'll be delighted to take up your suggestion of a trip to the mountains. Maybe we'll rent a cabin and stay the whole weekend."

"What's this?" a deep, husky voice interrupted. "My Miss Barnes is going on a weekend assignation?"

Color mounted in Grace's cheeks and she turned to greet Luc Salvatore, struggling to hang on to the cool, calm demeanor she'd perfected these past eleven months. "It was just a thought," she stated, forced to look a long way up to meet his golden gaze.

He stepped closer, trapping her against Edward's desk, an intent expression touching his handsome features. "Not a good one, if this blush is anything to go by." He ran a slow finger along her cheekbone, his broad shoulders eclipsing her view of anything else. He'd cut them off from the rest of the world, and it made her nervous. Very nervous. "No need to jump into these things if you aren't ready."

She heard the concern in his voice and her brows drew together. She felt like a heel, worrying Edward and Luc with a conversation about an imaginary romantic interlude with an equally imaginary fiancé. "Thanks for your advice," she said discouragingly, hoping to end this particular discussion before she got in any deeper.

"You're welcome." Cupping her elbow, Luc escorted her toward the elevators. "Why all this sudden talk about a weekend trip with what's-his-name?"

She shot him a look of annoyance. "His name is Will . . . William, as you know full well."

"And Will-William is dragging you off to his mountain lair to have his wicked way with you? Is that what you were telling Edward?"

"That's none of your business." She studiously faced the elevator doors, refusing to so much as glance his way. Not that it helped. The shiny gold doors acted as a mirror, reflecting the determination in his gaze. "And don't think I didn't see that look you and Edward exchanged," she added for good measure.

"It's my business if I choose to make it my business." He positioned himself in front of her, blocking the doors. "And what look are you referring to?"

She deliberately kept her attention fixed on the red silk tie knotted at his throat. As usual, it was slightly askew. And as usual, she valiantly resisted the temptation to straighten it. With each passing day, however, the temptation grew stronger.... One of these days she'd give in. If she was lucky, that would also be day three hundred and sixty-five on the job. "You know the look I mean. That significant man-to-man, women-are-such-fools one."

"Ah... You mean our look of mutual concern."

Her gaze flashed upward, locking with his. It was a mistake. He could melt ice with those eyes. Her annoyance didn't stand a chance—it evaporated like mist beneath a hot sun. "My personal life is none of your business," she managed to say. Finally succeeding in breaking eye contact, she addressed his tie once again. "And it is most certainly none of Edward's."

"On the contrary. You elected to share your personal life with Edward, so you have no one to blame but yourself if he offers an opinion." His long, lean fingers brushed her jaw, making her face him. "And whether you believe it or not, everything about you is my affair." He made the sweeping statement with such utter sincerity that it left no room for doubt.

Her breathing stopped. "Why would you care if Will... William and I went away for the weekend?" She still choked every time she uttered her fictitious fiancé's name. And Luc—darn him—took due note.

The elevator doors slid open and he stepped aside so they could enter. He keyed the lock for the top floor before responding. "Is he pressuring you?" Luc asked.

She knew exactly what he meant, but she lifted her chin and gave him a bland smile anyway. "Pressuring me? Whatever do you mean?"

He turned on her, disapproval carving his features into a stony mask. "To have sex, as you well know. And don't bother with that innocent expression and the coy lies. You're not good at it, Grace."

She fought to keep a straight face. Little did he know. Over the past year she'd become unbelievably adept at lying. And if her father ever found out, it would break his heart. "I refuse to discuss this matter further," she announced in no uncertain terms. "I repeat. It's none of your business."

He stabbed a button on the elevator and the car jerked to a stop. "Don't do it, Gracie," he urged in a husky voice. "Don't go away with him on a whim. You deserve better than that."

She glared at Luc, sick of her deception, wishing she could be herself instead of guarding every word she uttered. But she couldn't, and she forced herself to demand, "What could be better than a snow-covered mountain chalet buried deep in a redwood forest?"

His hands snagged the collar of her coat, rubbing the butter-soft wool along the length of her jaw. "For your first time...I think a second-floor suite at the Ritz in Paris overlooking the *Place Vendôme* would suit you best."

She stared at him in alarm. He'd never made such personal remarks before, never touched her like this or gazed down at her with such a smoldering expression. This sudden change in their relationship unsettled her. "Who said it would be my first time?" she asked weakly, an odd tension gathering in the pit of her stomach.

"I say," he replied.

She didn't dare argue the point. Not when he was right. Instead she maintained, "I happen to think snuggling with my fiancé in front of a roaring fire with nothing between me and a bearskin rug but a scrap of lace sounds perfect.'' She could hear the tension in her voice now, but for some reason she couldn't bring herself to end this strange and intimate conversation.

His eyes half closed and he bent closer, murmuring, ''Making love on top of dead animals doesn't appeal to me. And with your skin, nothing but silk will do. Something low cut and simple.'' He released her collar, the back of his hand stroking a leisurely path across her cheek and jaw. ''Better yet, why don't we try a feather mattress and nothing between us at all. What do you say to that?''

She shivered beneath his touch, horrified by the magnitude of her reaction to him. Where was her control? Where was her detachment? ''Luc...'' His name escaped on a breathless sigh.

His mouth curved upward. ''Is that a yes?''

Her eyes widened in panic and she inhaled sharply, fighting the desire that swept through her veins like wildfire. ''No!''

''Just checking,'' he said with an easy shrug. ''So good old Will-William the accountant from San Jose—''

''San Mateo!''

''—wants sex beside a roaring fire and is offering a chalet, champagne and dead animals to get his way. Is that about it?''

He hadn't been serious about making love to her, she realized then. He'd merely been teasing again. He didn't really care—not on a personal basis. The knowledge bit deep. It didn't matter what he thought of her, she tried to convince herself. It didn't. *It didn't!*

''Maybe,'' she said in a hard, tight voice, ''that isn't what he's offering, but what *I'm* offering.''

She pulled free and jabbed the button to resume the ride, but not before she saw anger flash across Luc's face. Good. Let him be on the losing side of a disagreement for once. She faced the elevator doors again, seeing her metallic reflection as he saw it.

She'd kept her hair rinsed to a nondescript shade of brown and still pinned it into a tight knot at the nape of her neck. The tinted glasses she wore had proved most effective, swamping her delicate features, concealing her leaf green eyes and high-boned cheeks. Her experiments with makeup only added insult to injury. The foundation she'd chosen gave her face a pallid, sallow appearance. And completing her disguise were her clothes, the businesslike suits a size too large and ranging in tone from a dirt brown to navy and black.

It was absolutely perfect.

It also made her want to cry.

This past year had given her an acute awareness of how cruel the world could be toward unattractive people. All her father's little sermons about vanity, about it being a person's inner beauty that counted most, came home to roost. Never again would she ever judge by appearances alone.

"I didn't mean to upset you," Luc said at last. "I'm sorry."

"That's quite all right," she replied in a stilted voice. And though she'd just vowed to never again judge by appearances, she couldn't help wishing—wishing with a passion that shocked her—that he could see her as she really was.

The elevator slowed and the doors opened. Blocking her avenue of escape, he said, "But you still shouldn't sleep with him unless you're sure. Very sure."

He stepped off the elevator, leaving her openmouthed and fuming. Before she could dart between the doors, they closed with a snap, forcing her to endure a return trip to the lobby. Just as well, she decided with stoic resolve, since she'd left her umbrella leaning against Edward's desk.

Five minutes later, she arrived back on the executive floor and hurried to the reception area outside Luc's office. She disposed of her coat and umbrella in the office closet and sat at her desk. Removing a bright red marker from her drawer, she took even more than her usual delight in crossing one more day off her year-long sentence.

She looked up to see Luc standing at his door, watching.

"You do that every morning," he observed. "It's almost as though you were counting the days until..." He shrugged. "Something."

She stared at him, stricken. "Nonsense."

His eyes narrowed. "It's not nonsense. What are you counting down to?"

"Nothing!" Had she somehow given herself away? She couldn't have!

"That's twice today," he stated ominously.

She swallowed. "Twice?"

"Twice today you've lied to me."

He frowned and she froze. His frowns, rare though they were, worried her. A lot. They invariably preceded an explosion. Only once had that explosion been directed her way, and she'd decided then and there it would be the last time she'd give him cause to exercise that infamous temper of his.

"I don't like it, Grace," he said softly, a certain menace marking his voice. "Don't lie to me again."

She didn't dare respond, didn't dare dwell on what would happen should he discover the deception she and Dom had instigated—especially considering it was aimed directly at Luc. She could only pray he didn't find out. Because if he ever did . . . She shuddered.

So, what had tipped him off about her latest fibs? And why weren't they working today? She thought she'd gotten rather good at evading the truth, but perhaps months and months of practicing such a bad habit had caused a sort of short circuit and she was all lied out. Or perhaps Luc's dislike of them had finally rubbed off on her.

Her father would be delighted, were he to know. Grace was horrified.

Luc didn't wait for an answer, which was a relief since she had none to offer. Instead, he returned to his office and closed the door with gentle emphasis. She stared blindly at her calendar. Four more weeks. That's all she had to get through. Just four more weeks.

In just under three of those weeks Dom Salvatore would return from his year-long sojourn to Italy and appoint a relative to take over as Luc's assistant. One quick week of training and Grace would be free to open Baby Dream Toys. Her dearest wish—her mother's dearest wish—would finally be realized.

She focused on the calendar. She could do it. Just four more weeks of lies and half-truths, disguises and evasions. What could be easier? The problem was, would she still think it worthwhile once she had her shop? She'd worried about this at length. When she'd first agreed to Dom's plan, she'd wanted her own business so badly that she hadn't paused to weigh the consequences. She'd had plenty of time since to reconsider her hasty and ill-planned decision. And now she wasn't so sure she'd made the right choice. Using deceit to attain her goal, even when it was a lifelong dream, went against the grain.

She was living a lie. And she'd never been more uncomfortable in her life. Worse, she liked working for Luc. He was a fantastic employer—generous, intelligent, creative. She'd even found their frequent battle of wills challenging. If not for the lies, it would be the perfect job.

A small sound caught her attention, and looking up, Grace noticed a beautiful young woman standing in the doorway of the reception area. She carried a huge diaper bag over one arm; in the other she clutched a baby.

"May I help you?" Grace asked, shoving her glasses higher on her nose.

The young woman shot Grace a suspicious glance, then shook her head. She peered around rather frantically. When her gaze landed on Luc's door and the plaque that read *Luciano Salvatore,* she let out an exclamation of relief. Eyeing Grace with a measure of defiance, she sidled toward Luc's door.

Grace stood. This did not look too encouraging. A young woman, infant in arms, acting as though Luc's door held the answer to all her prayers... "Excuse me, but do you have an appointment?" she asked, though she could guess the answer to that one. This little entrance had "surprise visit" written all over it. Her hands closed into fists. How would Luc take to his newly discovered papahood? she wondered in despair. She already knew how *she* felt about it, the sick, sinking feeling in the pit of her stomach all too clear an indication.

More to the point... when had her feelings for Luc changed? When had she begun to care?

There was no mistaking the young woman's resolve. She glanced from Grace to the door as though judging her chances of winning a footrace. As Grace came around the desk, determination glittered in the woman's huge sloe eyes and she literally threw herself at Luc's door. Yanking it open, she launched into a spate of very loud Italian and slammed the door in Grace's face.

Grace's mouth fell open.

"Miss Barnes!" Luc's roar rattled the rafters an instant later. "Get in here!"

It took her a split second to gather her wits sufficiently to obey. Then she, too, charged the door and threw it open. Mother and infant had found sanctuary in Luc's arms, and between sobs the woman poured out what appeared to be a most heartrending story. Luc fired a quick question and the woman stepped back, her Italian loud and furious. Startled from a sound sleep, the baby burst into tears, his wails competing with his mother's.

"You bellowed?" Grace asked.

He stabbed a finger at her. "Don't start. Go down the hall and drag my brother Pietro out of his office. I want him in here. Now."

She turned to leave, only to discover Pietro standing behind her. "What's all the shouting?" he asked, then took one look at the woman at Luc's side and cried, "Carina!"

The sudden realization that the child was, in all probability, Pietro's and not Luc's, grabbed Grace's full attention. Fighting to ignore an overwhelming sense of relief, she slipped farther into the room, watching this latest development with intense interest.

Pietro crossed to Carina's side and started to take her into his arms. Grace could tell the instant he noticed the baby. It took precisely two seconds for the significance to sink in. "What the hell is this?" he shouted.

"What does it look like?" Carina shouted back. "It is a baby."

The infant in question started crying again. Grace, realizing the door to Luc's office stood open, turned to close it. A gaggle of secretaries had gathered in a loose semicircle, listening with open mouths. "I'll get security," one of them offered, and darted down the hallway before Grace could stop her. With a sigh, she shut the door. One problem at a time.

"Enough!" Luc thundered. "I want quiet and I want it now!" To Grace's astonishment, all obeyed, even the baby. "Excellent. Now. Do you think we could get to the bottom of this mess?"

"Fine. Your brother, he is a pig!" Carina condemned, then broke into a long litany of passionate Italian.

"English, please," Luc requested.

"My English, it is not so good."

"Really? Pietro's Italian is even worse." He eyed the baby grimly. "I see you managed to overcome the language barrier despite that small obstacle. I think introductions are in order. Don't you?"

"Luc," Pietro spoke up. "This is Carina Donati. Carina, my brother Luciano and his assistant, Miss Barnes."

"Buon giorno," Carina acknowledged them with an abrupt nod.

"Carina and I... Well, we met at UC Berkeley," Pietro confessed. "She's a foreign-exchange student."

"Not any more," she interrupted, hugging the baby to her breast. "Now I am statistic. Unwed mother."

Pietro turned on her. "And whose fault is that?"

"Yours!" She offered him the baby. "You do not believe you are the papa?"

His hands balled into fists. "I damn well better be!"

"Children . . ." Luc inserted softly.

Grace crossed the room and held out her arms. "Why don't I take the baby?" she suggested, hoping to remove the poor infant from the field of battle. To her relief, Carina handed over her bundle without a single protest, and Grace retreated to the far side of the room.

Pietro addressed Carina, speaking at a more moderate level. "I phoned. You wouldn't answer any of my calls. I came over to the house. They said you'd moved out and hadn't left a forwarding address. I went everywhere I could think of to find you. It was like you'd vanished off the face of the earth."

Carina planted her hands on her curvaceous hips, scorn flashing in her magnificent eyes. "Of course I vanished. You lied to me!"

"I never!"

"What about Giovanna Carducci?"

"You left me because of Giovanna Carducci?"

Pathetic tears filled her eyes and she pointed a trembling finger. "See! He admits it."

"I'm not admitting anything!"

"That's enough," Luc interrupted once again. "Let me see if I have this straight. You and Carina met, fell in love, had a falling out over someone named Giovanna Carducci—"

"No!" Pietro denied.

"*Sì!*" Carina insisted.

"*And,*" Luc seized control of the conversation once more, "unbeknownst to Pietro, Carina conceived..." He gestured toward Grace and the baby.

"Tony," Carina supplied.

"Tony. Does that about cover it?"

"*Sì,*" Carina agreed. "In a nut case."

"Nutshell," Pietro corrected.

She tossed her hair over her shoulder. "Whatever it is, I don't care. The big man, he is right."

The "big man" sighed. "I hesitate to ask this, Carina, but you now want...what?"

As though on cue, the tears reappeared. Pietro took one look and pulled her into his arms. "Darling, what is it? What's happened?"

"My mother in Italy, she is very sick," Carina confessed, her voice breaking. "I must go to her. But I cannot."

Pietro stared at her in bewilderment. "Why not?"

She pulled free, glaring at him. "Why not? You look at my sweet, little Tony and ask, why not? I come from a very small village. My relatives are old-fashioned. If they ever find out I have a baby with no husband, I would be disowned. So I come up with solution."

"Which is?" Luc asked.

The tears finally escaped, sliding down her cheeks. With a cry of distress, she snatched Tony from Grace and repeatedly kissed the tuft of black hair peeking out of the blanket. Then Carina thrust the tiny bundle at Pietro. "Tony is also yours," she said, choking on a sob. "You take care of our baby while I am in Italy. When my mama is better, I will return and be an unwed, deserted mother once more." Dropping the diaper bag to the ground, she pushed past Grace and fled the room.

"Wait!" Pietro called. He started to follow, then realized he was somewhat encumbered.

"We need to discuss this," Luc began.

"Later." Pietro fumbled awkwardly with his armload and shot his brother a look of anguished pleading. "I have to stop her!"

"Mr. Salvatore?" Edward filled the doorway. "Is there a problem?"

"Yes, there is," Luc said. "Call down to the front desk. There's a young woman, petite, long dark hair, and probably crying. I want her detained. She's..." He glanced at the baby. "She's left behind a rather important package."

"Right away, sir," Edward agreed, and disappeared.

Luc turned back to his brother. "Pietro—"

"No! There isn't time." Without further ado, Pietro dumped the baby into Luc's arms. "You watch Tony. I'll go get Carina."

"Wait a minute! Come back here!" But it was too late. Pietro was gone. Luc stared in dismay at the baby, then glanced at Grace. A suspicious gleam appeared in his eyes. "Why, Miss Barnes," he practically purred, advancing toward her with his most charming—and determined—smile. He held out the baby. "Look what I have for you."

CHAPTER TWO

The Great Lie
Still Day 337 and all is not so well...

GRACE HELD UP HER HANDS and backed away. "Oh, no," she protested. "This is your problem."

Luc stopped dead in his tracks, staring in astonishment. "You'd desert me in my hour of need?"

"Yes."

"You'd leave Pietro and Carina in the lurch?" he demanded in disbelief.

"Without question."

His brows drew sharply together. "You'd turn your back on a poor, helpless baby?"

She stared at him, stricken. He'd gotten her with that one. She adored children. She always had. Throughout her teen years, when anyone had needed a baby-sitter, they'd called her. When the church needed someone to supervise the nursery on Sundays, her name was the first one mentioned. And though she wasn't terribly experienced with babies, she was still an easy touch when it came to their welfare.

"That's not fair," she complained. But he had her. And if he didn't know it, he undoubtedly sensed it.

"Come, *cara mia*." He held out Tony and offered a helpless smile. "I know nothing of babies. Besides, it won't be for long. Only until Pietro returns with Carina and they sort out their little problem."

Unable to resist, she took the "little problem" and peered into his sweet, sleeping face. Luc leaned over, running a long finger across the baby's flushed cheek.

"He's a Salvatore, all right," Luc pronounced. "He's the image of my brother."

"What's going to happen with Pietro and Carina?" she asked in concern.

"They'll marry." His golden eyes reflected his amusement. "It promises to be a rather volatile relationship, wouldn't you agree?"

She shuddered. "Too volatile." A far more serious question troubled her, and she gathered her nerve to voice it. "How will your father take the news?"

"Not well," Luc admitted. "He's as old-fashioned as Carina's parents." He smoothed the tiny line forming on Grace's brow, his touch easing her distress and yet fermenting a strange agitation. "Don't worry. I'll handle him. The first order of business is to get them married. That should go a long way toward placating my father."

"Perhaps you could be a little vague about the exact wedding date," Grace suggested. "Not lie, of course."

His lips curved. "No, we'd never lie, would we?"

She ducked her head. "Never," she agreed in a muffled voice. "But if we were to omit one or two minor details...?" She peeked up to see how he took to the suggestion.

He shrugged, his expression unreadable. "We'll play it by ear. Let's hope that seeing his very first grandchild will temper my father's reaction."

She gnawed at her lower lip. "He...he wouldn't throw Pietro out of the family, would he?" She'd known parents who'd done that over far less serious infractions. But not Dom. He was the sweetest, most benevolent man she'd ever met. Surely he wouldn't overreact to such an extent. He had to realize it could tear his entire family apart if he were to disown Pietro. And she knew for a fact that family meant everything to him.

"He might," Luc acknowledged grimly, confirming her worst fears. "He has very strong opinions about this sort of thing. And his opinion is...it doesn't happen. Period."

She stared at Luc in alarm. "But—"

He dropped a casual arm around Grace's shoulders and gave her a reassuring hug. "Relax," he said, his touch once again arousing a strange, disturbing flutter deep in her stomach. "You're not to worry. I'll take care of everything. Trust me."

Grace nodded, believing him. If there was one thing she'd learned about Luc, it was that he did precisely what he promised. If he said he'd take care of Dom, then he'd take care of Dom. As far as trusting him... She stared at Luc, stared at the lean, chiseled features that reflected his strength and power, and at the direct, golden eyes, so full of confidence and determination. Slowly, she relaxed.

She'd trust him with her life.

He released her, crossing to the large built-in cabinet on the far side of the room. "Let's see what's happening downstairs," he said, folding back the cabinet doors and revealing a bank of monitors inside. Switching them on, he called up a view from the security camera in the lobby and put it on the large center screen. "There's Pietro and Carina. I don't see Edward, yet. I wonder what's taking him so long?"

"He must have gotten delayed in the elevator," Grace murmured, crossing to stand beside him. "Oh, dear. They're arguing again."

"That's not arguing. That's shrieking."

She frowned, cuddling the baby. "Maybe you should go down there and mediate."

After a momentary hesitation, he shook his head. "Pietro wouldn't thank me if I butted in. He's made it clear over the past year that he prefers taking care of his own problems without big brother's interference. He'll call if he needs help."

"You're sure?"

"No."

"No!" She spun to stare at him. "Did you say no?"

"I said no."

"That doesn't exactly make me feel any better," she pointed out.

He shrugged. "Considering how stubborn Pietro can be, it's the best I can offer."

"It would seem stubbornness is a Salvatore trait." She switched her attention back to the monitor. "I wish we could hear what's going on. I don't suppose you read lips."

He gave a short laugh. "I don't need to. It's obvious what they're saying. Pietro's yelling, 'Why didn't you tell me about Tony?'"

Grace allowed herself a brief smile, despite her concern. "And Carina is shouting back, 'Why should I have?'"

He slanted her a quick look, a spark of humor glittering in his eyes. "Because I'm the father of your baby."

Her smile widened. "So?"

"So, you shouldn't have hidden my son from me." He shifted closer. "I had a right to know about him."

Getting into the role, she replied, "You have no rights as far as I'm concerned. You betrayed me. You had an affair with...*her.*"

Luc slipped an arm around Grace's waist. "That other woman means nothing to me, *mia amorata*," he murmured, his mouth practically brushing her cheek.

She shivered, fighting the urge to return his embrace, fighting the sharp desire that intensified with every passing moment. How had this happened? How had this attraction managed to slip past her guard with such stunning ease. And why now, when she was so close to attaining her dream? She struggled to remember the role she played. "The . . . the other woman . . ."

"You're the only woman I care about, the only woman I—"

"Don't say it," she cut in sharply, tumbling out of her role with a vengeance. "Not unless you mean it. Because I know you don't care. Not really."

"I do."

She shook her head. "No. You love all women. I'm just one of many."

"You're right. I admit it. I do love women." He, too, had dropped the playacting, she realized, his eyes darkening, losing their glint and turning serious. Deadly serious. "I love all women, young and old, short and tall, with dark hair scraped back in a bun or with long blond hair left loose around the shoulders. They are all beautiful to me."

She gazed up at him in alarm, resisting the urge to touch her hair. Nervously, she licked her lips and whispered, "Then you admit it?"

His index finger brushed her lower lip, the caress fleeting yet potent. "I admit only that I love all women. I love the diversity of their appearance. I love the unique scent of a woman—musky or flowery or as fresh as the first breath of spring. I love to listen to them speak, how one will sound rough and smoky and another as smooth as thick maple syrup. I love to watch them move, all long limbed and coltish or tiny dynamos bustling with energy. But my favorites are those who dance to some inner music only they can hear, supple and graceful and filled with the joy of living . . . like you.''

She shook her head. "No . . . Don't say any more.''

But he didn't stop. Instead his hands cupped her shoulders, his thumbs stroking the sensitive hollow of her throat. "Did you know that touching a woman is one of life's greatest joys? To explore each silken curve and feel the hot rush of her passion, to hold her in your arms and know that your touch brings her to life.''

She wanted to jerk away, but she couldn't. Not while hampered by the baby...hampered by her reaction to his words, his touch. "Luc, you shouldn't be saying these things to me,'' she insisted weakly.

"But I haven't told you the best part about women. Do you know what it is?'' He didn't wait for her answer. "It's their taste. The taste of a woman is a gift from the gods. It's headier than the finest wine and more intoxicating than the strongest rum. And it only improves with age . . . and with experience.''

She shut her eyes, afraid to look at him, afraid of the passion she read in his face. "You're forgetting about Pietro and Carina,'' she whispered, knowing she should be watching the monitor but unable to tear her gaze from Luc's.

"I haven't forgotten them,'' he murmured. "You accuse me of loving women. And I admit my guilt. You're right. I do love women. But how I feel about them is nothing—absolutely nothing—compared with how I feel about you.''

She shook her head, holding Tony tight to her breast. "You tell such sweet lies, beautiful lies. But that's all they are—lies. Women fascinate you. You find them irresistible. Too irresistible to ever settle on just one."

"You're wrong." His voice was deep and husky, the underlying lilt more pronounced than ever. "Once a Salvatore falls in love, it's for ever. He never strays."

She forced herself to look at him again, to try and judge the degree of honesty in his expression. "I—I don't believe you."

"Yes, you do, because it's the truth. Salvatores never stray. Never." Then he released her and stepped back. "And that, *cara mia,* is what Pietro is saying to Carina. It's what I'd say in his place to the woman I loved."

Grace blinked, the spell of words he'd cast slowly fading. She didn't know what to think, what to say... what to feel. Her gaze fell from his, and out of desperation she focused on the monitor. "Luc, look!"

Carina and Pietro were no longer arguing. Action seemed to be the order of the day. Gesturing wildly, Carina grabbed a huge porcelain vase from off a pedestal beside the front door and dumped the contents over the top of Pietro's head. Water, gladioli and bits of fern dripped from his shoulders and puddled on the floor.

Grace winced. "I guess his explanation wasn't as smooth as yours," she murmured.

"I guess not. But she shouldn't have done that," Luc said with a sigh. "He's not going to take it at all well."

Sure enough, Pietro exploded, gesturing wildly. Just then, Edward appeared on the scene. Eyes practically popping out of his head, he attempted to brush the flower petals and pieces of greenery from Pietro's suit.

"I wish Carina would put that vase down," Grace said, shifting Tony to her shoulder.

"It's *where* she'll put it down that worries me."

No sooner had he said that, than Edward endeavored to wrest the vase from Carina's hands. For a few tense seconds they tussled. Jerking it free, it flew from Edward's hands and crashed against the side of Pietro's head. He went down like a ton of bricks.

Luc raced for a phone and called down to the security desk. "Call the staff doctor to help Pietro. Fast! I'll be right there."

"Luc, wait! You better check this out first," Grace called in a panic. "It doesn't look good."

They could no longer see Pietro. A huge crowd had gathered around him, blocking the view. Off to one side, security men were converging on Carina, who wept copiously. Far worse, two police officers came bursting through the front doors. Carina looked from the security men to the police, and apparently decided the law was a safer bet than the furious employees of a stricken Salvatore. She darted to their side.

"I don't know what tale of woe she's spinning, but it's making quite an impression," Luc observed in disgust. "She'll be gone before I even reach the elevators. Yep. There she goes. Out the door, into the first cab that passes by and on her way to the airport."

"What about Pietro?" Grace asked in concern.

"Wait a sec. He's up." Luc relaxed slightly. "Thank heavens."

"He seems to be all right, but he could still have a concussion. I wish the doctor was there," Grace fussed. "Oh, no. Now he's yelling at the police."

"Probably for letting Carina go."

"Why does that policewoman have her handcuffs out? They're not going to arrest him, are they?" she questioned in alarm. "He hasn't done anything wrong."

"Except give the police a hard time, knowing Pietro. They tend to frown on that." He watched the screen, an intent expression on his face. "Good. They're releasing him."

"Great, except where's he going?" She pointed at the screen. "Now he's leaving the building, too."

"Damn!" Luc thrust a hand through his hair. "He's going after Carina. I should have guessed he'd pull something like that."

"But what about Tony? He can't expect us..." Her eyes widened in disbelief.

He smiled grimly and nodded. "Looks like we have baby-sitting duties until Pietro catches up with Carina."

"Oh, no. No way. Not a chance."

Before he could respond, the phone rang. Luc snatched it up. "Edward? How's Pietro? Yes, yes. I know he left. Where's he headed?" He covered the mouthpiece and spoke to Grace, "I was right. He's on his way to the airport. Hang on, Edward. I'm putting you on the speakerphone." He punched a button.

"Er...Mr. Salvatore? Can you hear me? This is Edward Rumple speaking. Over."

"We hear you," Grace said quickly. "Is Pietro all right? He isn't hurt too badly?"

"Just a goose egg, Miss Barnes. Hardly any blood at all." He cleared his throat. "But there is just one little problem."

"What is it, Edward?" Luc asked.

"Well, ah, you aren't going to like this, but..."

"Spit it out."

"Yes, sir, Mr. Salvatore. See, Mr. Pietro happened to mention the baby the young lady left behind and, ah, well, the truth is... To be perfectly honest..."

"Edward!"

"I thought I'd better warn you that—"

A loud pounding sounded on the outer door. "Police. Open up, please."

"—the police are on their way up," Edward finished lamely.

For an instant Luc didn't move. Then in a calm, collected voice, he said, "Thank you, Edward. Keep everything under control down there and notify me the instant Pietro returns. I'll deal with the police." Hanging up the phone, he crossed to the door.

"Luc?" Grace said uncertainly.

He spared her a brief glance. "It'll be okay. Just try not to look worried and let me do the talking." At her nod, he opened the door and held out his hand. "Hello. I'm Luc Salvatore, president of Salvatore Enterprises. What can I do for you—" he checked their name tags "—Officers Cable and Hatcher?"

"We're responding to a report of an abandoned infant," said Officer Cable. She glanced at the baby Grace held. "Is that the child?"

"This baby isn't abandoned," Luc stated firmly, moving to stand between Grace and the policewoman.

"No?" Officer Hatcher, a tall, sturdy man, stepped forward. "Is he yours?"

"He's my nephew."

The two officers exchanged quick glances. "I'm afraid we'll have to see some identification," Cable requested.

Grace could tell from their attitudes that they were taking this situation very, very seriously. Luc removed his driver's license from his wallet and handed it to the policewoman. "Perhaps an explanation is in order?" he suggested with a quick smile.

Grace waited for Officer Cable's reaction to that smile. It wasn't long coming. She fumbled for his license, ef-

fected a swift recovery, then made a production of re-
cording the information on her clipboard. A spot of color
appeared high on each cheekbone. Luc didn't even notice.

Grace sighed. But then, he never did. He'd bowl them
over like ninepins and never realize they'd fallen. To his
credit, it wasn't calculated. As Luc had admitted, he
simply loved women and treated every last one with a
devastating courtesy and warmth. It was, without question, his greatest charm.

"I think an explanation would be very helpful,"
Hatcher interrupted, keenly attuned to his partner's reaction. He strode across the room, firing a quelling
glance at Cable. Somewhat chagrined, she reverted to a
more professional demeanor.

"I believe you met my brother Pietro Salvatore downstairs," Luc began.

"He was the one involved in the altercation with the
young woman?"

"A small family squabble," Luc said dismissively.
"We're a very...emotional household."

"The young woman is...?"

"His wife."

Grace's mouth fell open at the blatant lie—the first
she'd ever heard him utter—and a tiny gasp escaped before she could prevent it. She stared at Luc in disbelief;
he never blinked an eye. Nor did he look at her. But Officer Hatcher did. Grace quickly shut her mouth and focused her attention on the baby, but she suspected it was
too little, too late. Sure enough, he approached.

"You have something to add, Miss..."

"Barnes. Grace Barnes. And yes, I do. Could...could
you hand me that diaper bag? I believe we've had a little
accident here," she murmured weakly.

The officer's eyes narrowed but he didn't call her a liar to her face, which came as a relief. He bent down and picked up the bag. She took it with a grateful smile and gently deposited the baby on top of Luc's desk, smack-dab in the center of his leather blotter. Serve him right if it was ruined, she decided. He shouldn't have lied to the police. She unwrapped the blanket around Tony and made a production of unsnapping the bottom of his jumper.

"To get back to the matter at hand," Officer Hatcher continued. "The young lady we questioned, her name is...?"

"Carina Donati...Salvatore," Luc replied.

"And she left to go to the airport?"

"Yes, her mother in Italy is very ill. My brother asked her to wait until they could all fly together, but she wanted to get home as soon as possible. I'm sorry you had to be involved." He shrugged. "It really wasn't necessary."

"About the baby," Officer Cable interrupted. "You've been left with the infant until your brother returns?"

"It's only for a few hours."

Grace kept her head down and removed a fresh diaper, wipes and powder from the bag. Sliding the rubber pants off Tony's plump, churning legs, she discovered to her relief that he was, indeed, wet. She unpinned the soggy diaper.

The officers conferred in low voices and she could tell they weren't comfortable with the situation. So could Luc, for he sighed. "Look. I'm a responsible man, respected in the community. I'm baby-sitting my nephew for a few hours. Why is that a problem?"

Grace slipped off the diaper, then glanced, wide-eyed, from the baby to Luc. Uh-oh. If she didn't move fast, something very nasty would hit the fan. Tossing the dirty diaper toward the trash can with one hand, she fumbled for a clean one with the other. To her horror, it slid to the floor.

"Would it help if I provided references?" Luc offered.

"You have someone who can vouch for your baby-sitting abilities?" Hatcher retorted. Clearly, he resented Cable's less-than-professional reaction to Luc and intended to make matters as difficult as possible. "You look like a busy man," he added, his gaze suspicious. "Are you sure you can provide adequate care?"

Grace saw the fierce expression on Luc's face and froze. That look did not bode well for any of them. He glanced at her with grim intent, then at her left hand and she knew, before he even moved, what he planned to do.

Without a moment to lose, she whipped a new diaper from the bag, dropping it across Tony's lower extremities the exact same instant Luc dropped a possessive arm around her shoulders. Fighting his embrace, she struggled to position the diaper and pin it.

"Cara," he muttered. "Let me show them."

"Not now!" she whispered frantically.

"Yes, now." He grabbed her left hand and held it out toward the police officers. "Perhaps I should have said my *fiancée* and I will be baby-sitting little Tony."

"Luc, the baby," Grace whispered. He frowned at her, and she snatched her hand from his grasp. "I have to finish changing...him."

Not daring to give the police time to come closer, she gave up on the pins. Yanking the rubber pants up the tiny, kicking legs and praying the diaper would stay in place for the next two minutes, she wrapped the blanket around the baby. Then she collapsed into Luc's chair, lifted Tony to her shoulder and began to pat the baby's back, as if a brisk burping commonly followed a diaper change.

"You're engaged?" Officer Cable asked, not hiding her disappointment. Hatcher shoved his hat to the back of his head and grinned.

Grace shot Luc a fulminating glare. "Yes," she admitted, forcing out the lie. "I am." Fortunately they didn't ask if she was engaged to Luc. Lying to the police came low on her list of ambitions in life—not that she hadn't lied anyway, considering she wasn't really engaged at all.

Officer Cable gave a philosophical shrug. "I guess it's a false alarm," she said to her partner.

Officer Hatcher wasn't so accommodating. "We'll be writing this up," he informed them, without question suspecting that several vital details had been omitted from their story. "Next time I come here—and I will be back—I'll be having words with the baby's parents."

"Of course," Luc agreed.

He escorted the police officers to the elevators, leaving Grace and Tony behind. The minute they were gone, Grace returned the baby to the desk and quickly and efficiently repaired the droopy diaper. Tony fussed through the entire procedure, undoubtedly annoyed at having to suffer the same fate twice in less than five minutes.

Luc appeared in the doorway. "What are you doing?" he asked.

"Changing the baby."

"Again?"

"Yes, again. I was in such a hurry the first time, I didn't get it right."

"Why—"

She turned on him. "Do you realize what would have happened if Officer Cable had come over while I was changing the baby?"

Amusement sparked in his eyes. "She would have seen how a baby gets changed?"

"She would have seen that Tony is actually Toni."

"Come again?"

"I mean...Toni isn't your nephew but your niece!" Grace snapped. She picked up the baby and carried her to the couch, nestling her safely among the cushions.

"What?"

Grace folded her arms across her chest. "Toni apparently stands for Antonia, not Antonio."

"You're kidding!" Luc grinned in amazement. "That's wonderful. She's the first female Salvatore in...in four generations. Or is it five?"

Grace struggled to control her temper. "You're missing the point. If the police had discovered that you didn't even know the sex of your brother's child, the whole game would have been up. They'd have thrown us both in jail and taken the baby into custody."

He shook his head. "I wouldn't have let them."

"You couldn't have prevented it!" She didn't remember when she'd last been so angry. "How dare you!"

He stood, leaning against the doorframe, watching her intently. "How dare I what?"

"How dare you lie to them! I mean, when you finally cut loose with a fib, it's a whopper. But did you *have* to start with the police?"

He shrugged. "It seemed...appropriate at the time."

"Great," she grumbled. "So why involve me in your family problems?"

He grabbed her shoulders, hauling her close. "*Our* problems," he reminded in a soft, deliberate voice.

"We're engaged. You even told the police that, remember?"

She shook her head frantically. "No. I...I didn't. I just agreed that I was engaged, not that I was engaged to—"

He cut her off. "That isn't how they'll recall the conversation."

"But, it's all a lie," she protested. "Every bit of it. I'm not engaged to you. Pietro and Carina are not married. Darn it, Luc, the baby's not even a him."

She saw the storm gathering in his eyes, saw the fury and determination lock his expression into a cold, taut mask. "Let me explain something to you. I will not allow the police or anyone else to take Toni from me. I will do anything, *anything,* to protect her."

She didn't doubt him for a minute. And she could even sympathize with his feelings. The Salvatores were a close, unified family—all for one and one for all had long been their credo. And if truth be known, she did feel a certain obligation to Luc. After all, hadn't she spent the past year lying to him? She...she *owed* him a lie. But only a small short-term one. After that, she'd consider them even.

"What do you want from me?" she asked warily.

He had her and he knew it. He relaxed, the fire in his eyes dying until the gold gleamed like banked embers. His grip relaxed into a caress. "Not much. I just want you to stay with me—posing as my fiancée should the need arise—until Carina or Pietro return."

"Two hours. That's all you get," she bargained.

"Not good enough. I need you until my brother picks up Toni."

"No."

He gave her a wounded look. "You'd desert me in my hour of need?"

"Yes."

"You'd leave Pietro and Carina in the lurch?"

"Without question. We've been through this before. Remember?"

"So we have," he agreed softly, releasing her. "I believe this is where I ask if you'd turn your back on a helpless baby. As I recall that seemed to make a difference last time."

She really, truly tried to refuse. But she couldn't. She couldn't desert Toni, no matter how mad she was at Luc. "You don't play fair," she complained.

"No," he agreed. He caught her hand in his and raised it to his lips in a graceful gesture. Then he smiled, a most charming, dangerous smile. "I play to win."

CHAPTER THREE

The Great Lie
Day 337 continues to worsen...

"NO, NO! THAT'S TOO MUCH. It says here three scoops of formula to *six* ounces of water. Dammit, Grace, now look what you've done. You've spilled it!"

"*I* spilled it?" Grace shoved a tumble of curls out of her eyes and glared at Luc. "*You* jostled my arm."

"Well, your arm was in my way. This time watch what you're doing or you'll knock it to the..." The bottle clattered to the ground, milk soaking into the rug.

"Floor?" she inserted with a long-suffering sigh.

"Get another bottle. This one's contaminated. We'll have to start over."

"We can't."

He planted his hands on his hips. "And why not?" he demanded aggressively.

"Simple," she retorted, struggling to remain cool, calm and collected in the face of staggering odds— namely one Luc Salvatore. "We're out of bottles."

"Not for long." He marched to the phone, snatched it from the cradle and punched some buttons. "Edward? We're out of bottles. Order up another batch. And send out for more formula, too. Grace has gone clumsy on me."

"How could I have ever thought he was charming?" she muttered, struggling to repin her hair in its customary knot. "Charming, in a pig's eye. I must have been out of my mind."

He slapped his hand over the receiver. "What's that? Did you say something?"

"I said, make sure he gets the right kind."

"Edward. Make sure you get the right kind of formula. Grace is afraid you'll screw up again."

She raced to the phone and yanked it from his hand. "Edward? It's Grace. I did *not* say that. I didn't even think it. Hello? Hello?"

Luc lifted his finger off the plunger. "Hang up on you, did he?"

She returned the phone to its cradle and confronted him, poking her glasses higher up the bridge of her nose. "That was really low, even for you. And considering how much you need my help, I suggest—"

"Shh. The baby, remember?" As though in response, a tiny squawk drifted from across the room. "Uh-oh. Too late." He folded his arms across his chest and regarded her accusingly. "*You* made her cry."

"Ohh. I ought to—"

"Temper, temper." He grabbed for the phone again, raking a hand through his hair as he dialed. "Edward! Edward, she's crying.... What? How do I know? I haven't been a baby for years. Oh, really? No, kidding. Diapers or bottles, you say?"

Grace winced at the sarcasm. Time to take matters into her own hands. She headed out of Luc's office and into the reception area. Luc's voice drifted to her through the open door.

"That might prove a little difficult since you haven't sent any up! And another thing—"

She settled a hip on the edge of her desk and lifted the extension phone. "Edward? It's Grace. Just so you know, I did not say I thought you might screw anything up. I want that clearly on the record."

"Yes, Miss Barnes," Edward said with a deep sigh.

She opened her steno pad. "Now. You've ordered the correct formula? It has to be exactly like the can Carina left. The one with extra iron."

"Yes, Miss Barnes."

"He's not an idiot, Grace. He's not going to make the same mistake twice," Luc informed her. "Are you, Edward?"

"No, Mr. Salvatore."

"Luc, hang up. I can handle this."

"Like you handled the bottle and formula?"

"That wasn't my fault! Hello? Hello?"

"He hung up, Miss Barnes."

"Oh. Well, good. Let's see ... What else do we need? Here it is. We must have those sterilized bottles as soon as you can get them." She made a quick notation, then asked, "And what about diapers? We're almost out. Perhaps disposable would be a good bet."

"What size?"

That stopped her. "Small?"

"They go by weight."

Grace nibbled on her lip. "I'll have to get back to you on that."

"Yes, Miss Barnes."

"Damnation!" The shout came from Luc's office. "Grace? Grace! Get in here, quick!"

"Gotta go, Edward."

"I couldn't be that lucky."

"Grace!"

She frowned. "What was that, Edward?"

"I said, er, that would be just ducky."

Luc appeared in the doorway. "Get off that phone. Now. And get in here. There's something wrong with Toni."

Without another word, she hung up and hurried after him. He crossed to the makeshift crib they'd constructed out of couch cushions and winter coats. "What is it?" she asked, standing beside him and peering down at the baby. "What's wrong?"

"Look at her," he ordered. "She's foaming at the mouth. That's bad, right? Don't they shoot you when you do that?"

"She's blowing bubbles," Grace explained. "At three months, we say it's cute. We frown on it when a child turns six. At thirteen, a stern reprimand is in order. It's only bubble-blowing adults we shoot."

"You're certain?"

"Absolutely. Now for the next problem."

He relaxed. "You mean the problem of getting any work done today?"

"No. The problem of diapers."

"I'll call Edward—"

"No, you won't. I've already spoken to him about it and we need to know what size to order."

"Small. Very small," Luc decided promptly.

She flashed him a superior look. "It goes by weight."

"Light. Very light."

Her lips twitched, and an instant later Luc laughed, a low, rumbling sound that drew her in and before she knew it, forged yet another bond of intimacy between them. Unable to resist, she laughed, too. "This is crazy, isn't it?" she asked with a wide, open smile.

"But fun. I have a niece. That's a nice feeling."

He slid an arm around Grace's shoulders, tucking her close, and together they stared down at Toni. It was a comfortable fit. Too comfortable. She should move away. But she didn't want to. With a tiny sigh, Grace gave in to the companionable mood and accepted his embrace. Hardly aware of what she did, she snuggled her head into the crook of his arm and relaxed her curves into his angles.

Just for this moment, she'd let down her guard and enjoy what the gods offered. It didn't mean anything. She knew better than to take it seriously. But right now, after all she'd been through, she needed his touch as much as she needed food and drink. Maybe even more.

"Listen..." His head bent closer to hers. "What's she doing now?" he whispered.

"She's cooing," Grace whispered back, shivering at the warm brush of his breath across her face.

"What does cooing mean? Is she hungry or is she wet?"

"I think it means she's happy," she murmured.

"Ah... Happy. That's good."

"Yes. Yes, it's very good. Happy is excellent." She turned into his arms and looked up at him, the strangely intense expression on his face catching her by surprise. Her hands clenched. "Luc..."

"Yes, Grace?"

"We need diapers." Somehow she'd managed to gather a fistful of his shirt, clinging to him as though her life depended on it. Self-consciously, she splayed her hands across his chest, smoothing out the wrinkles she'd created, her fingers lingering on the hard ridge of muscle beneath.

He shook his head. "I don't need diapers. I do need something—and I need it very badly. But let me assure you, it's not diapers."

Hot color flooded her face. "I mean, the baby needs diapers. Toni. She needs them. Not you. I know that you don't."

"Very observant. Though if you keep rubbing my chest like that, you'll find out precisely what it is I *do* need."

She jumped back as though scalded. "I didn't mean to—it was an accident."

"Let me guess. You confused me with Will-William."

Horror filled her. How could she have been so foolish? How could she have let her defenses down for even one tiny second? She knew what Luc was like. She knew how dangerous he could be. And yet she'd allowed him to touch her. Worse, she'd touched him back.

"It won't happen again," she said stiltedly.

He stepped closer. "What won't? Your confusing me with Will-William or your rubbing my chest?"

"Neither. I didn't mean to—to," she gestured wildly, "you know."

He smiled. "To what?"

She hated him. She absolutely loathed him for putting her in such an awkward position. "*Touch* you, all right? I didn't mean to touch you. And I'm perfectly well aware that you're not Will . . . William."

A grim smile flickered across his mouth. "You can't even say his name without stumbling over it, can you? What sort of relationship is that?"

"William. William. William. There. Are you satisfied now?" She took a deep breath, struggling to curb her sudden spurt of anger. It wouldn't do to lose her temper around Luc. She'd never keep everything under control that way. Lifting her chin as though daring him to say anything further, she asked, "Could we please get back to the issue at hand? Diapers for Toni, remember?"

For a minute she thought he'd argue the point. In the past few months he'd become very concerned about her relationship with the nonexistent William. She could tell, just from his tense, combative stance, that he wanted to push the discussion back onto a personal note. And she'd do just about anything to avoid that.

"It's been a rather stressful day," she said. "We're both worried."

"And we don't want to say anything we might regret, is that what you're suggesting?"

"Yes. That's what I'm suggesting."

"In that case—" he reached down and scooped Toni into his arms "—let's get the diaper situation taken care of. Follow me."

He strode from the office and headed for the elevators. After a momentary hesitation, she followed. Within five seconds, he'd collected a swarm of oohing and ahhing secretaries. To Grace's disgust, they darted around him like bees desperate for pollen. He took it as his due, beaming proudly, as if he and he alone were responsible for Toni's adorable perfection. The elevator arrived and he excused himself from the chattering horde. Snagging Grace's elbow, he ushered her into the car and pushed the button for the basement.

"Where are we going?" she asked, her tone sharper than she'd intended. Great. Just great. Give him something more to comment on. Just what she needed.

"We're going to the mail room," he answered in a suspiciously bland tone of voice.

"Why are we going to the mail room?"

"Wait and see. But be prepared to be impressed."

"I can hardly contain myself."

"Try," he suggested dryly.

Exiting the elevator, he led the way through the carpeted hallways to the enormous mail room. All work ceased the moment he walked into the place, but Luc didn't even seem to notice. He crossed to one of the desks and gently placed his precious bundle in the middle of a postage scale.

"Twelve pounds, eleven and one half ounces," he announced with satisfaction. "Grace, order the diapers."

"Okay. I admit it," she said with a sigh. "I'm impressed."

His expression serious, he leveled an intense, dark gaze at her. "Not yet, you aren't. But give it time. Because before long I intend to impress the hell out of you."

She could only stare at him, her breath fast and furious, her eyes huge. "What are you talking about?" she finally managed to ask.

His gaze turned enigmatic. But "Time will tell," was all he'd say.

With no comeback to offer, she went to the nearest phone and put a call through to Edward. Then they returned upstairs. Within thirty minutes sterilized bottles, formula and disposable diapers filled the reception area. Fifteen minutes after that, Grace settled into Luc's leather couch with a fresh and sweet-smelling Toni and popped a bottle into the baby's tiny puckered mouth. Snuggling into the deep, soft cushions, Grace kicked off her shoes and put up her feet.

Luc looked over at her. "Comfortable?" he asked.

"Very."

"Good. Sit there and relax. I'm going to try and clear up some of this backlog." He reached for the first file off the stack of work piled on his desk.

"Great idea," she said sleepily. "You know something?"

He spared her a brief glance. "What?"

"As exhausting as it is playing mommy, I've decided that there's nothing more special in all the world than cradling this little piece of heaven in my arms." She yawned.

He leaned back in his chair, tapping his pen against his blotter, his expression hooded. "I can think of one other thing just as special," he replied.

"Can you?" She considered.

Maybe being held in a pair of strong, protective arms by the man you loved could match it. But she wasn't about to admit that to Luc. Even imagining such a thing was dangerous. And yet... Too tired to fight the wayward thought, she allowed her imagination free rein. Beautiful, delicious and utterly impossible images filled her head, and with a tiny, secretive smile, she drifted off to sleep.

"GRACE, WAKE UP."

"Go away," she protested in a muffled voice.

"Wake up, *cara mia*. It's time to go home."

"Home?" That penetrated. With a groan, she sat up, then gasped in horror. "The baby! I fell asleep—"

"Take it easy, sweetheart. Toni's fine. I slipped her out of your arms the minute you nodded off."

She sat up, the image of Luc watching her sleep an uncomfortable one. "What time is it?"

"Six."

"Six! Is Pietro back?"

"No."

"What about Carina?"

He shook his head. "Afraid not."

She shoved her hair out of her eyes and twitched her skirt hem down over her knees. Her disguise was rapidly falling apart. If she weren't careful, all of Dom's fine plans would soon come undone. Had Luc noticed anything unusual? She searched his face. Responding to her scrutiny, he lifted an eyebrow in question.

"Something must have happened to them," she said. "It doesn't take this long to get to and from the airport. They should be back by now."

"They had a lot to discuss." He shrugged. "Pietro knows Toni's safe with us. We'll hear from them soon."

Right on cue, the phone rang and Luc glanced over his shoulder. "My private line."

"Thank heavens," she whispered, knowing that only family used that number.

He crossed to his desk and snatched up the phone. "Pietro? Where the *hell* are you?" He listened for several minutes, then switched to Italian. Not that it mattered. From the anger in his voice, Grace knew this discussion didn't bode well for her future. "I want an update tomorrow, you understand?" he finally said. "Or I go to Father with this." He slammed down the phone.

Night had fallen and only a small desk lamp illuminated the room. Luc thrust his chair away from his desk and stood, crossing to the window behind him. San Francisco lay sprawled below, the city lights glittering through the misty rain.

"Good news?" she joked uneasily.

He wasn't amused. "Pietro missed Carina at the airport, as I'm sure you've surmised."

"When is he coming for Toni?"

"Not tonight." He turned to face her, deep shadows cutting across his face and concealing his expression. "And not tomorrow night."

"What—what does that mean?"

"It means we're in for a longer haul than I antici-pated." He moved into the light and she caught her breath as she discerned the full extent of his displeasure. "Pietro was calling from a plane phone. He's followed Carina to Italy."

From across the room, the baby let out a loud wail.

Grace hurried to Toni's side and picked her up. "You said it, sweet pea," she muttered, hugging the baby. Un-easily she recalled her promise—to stay until Carina or Pietro returned for Toni. She peeked nervously at Luc. From his cold, calculating look, he hadn't forgotten, ei-ther.

She closed her eyes and shivered. Oh, Lord. What had she let herself in for?

"GRACE. THE DOOR. NOW."

"If you'd move out of my light, I'd get it open a lot faster. For such a ritzy apartment complex, they sure don't light the hallways very well."

"Grace..." His tone held an implacable warning. "If you don't hurry up, I'm going to drop the strained spin-ach and squash surprise all over our feet."

Grace blew a loose curl of hair out of her eyes and fo-cused on the door to his apartment—and the stubborn lock that kept her on the wrong side of that door. "I told you when we were at the grocery store not to get the strained spinach and squash surprise. Babies this young don't eat strained spinach and squash surprise. They drink milk, and some eat flaked cereal."

"I wanted to be prepared, just in case."

She gave up on trying to work the key while holding a squirming baby. "In case, what? In case Toni gets a sud-den craving for big-boy beans and peachy peaches?"

"Dammit, Grace!" Luc peered into the bags. "I think I forgot the peaches."

"Oh, dear. I'm crushed. And look at Toni. She's crushed, too."

"The only one in danger of being crushed is me. You'd better get that door open fast or—" The bottom of one of the bags ripped and jars tumbled to the floor. Luc let fly with a very nasty word.

"Is that any way to speak in front of an innocent baby?" Grace demanded in disgust.

"Yes!" he snarled. "That's exactly how I speak in front of an innocent baby, when fifty pounds' worth of baby food jars have just nailed my big toe."

"I told you—"

"I know. I know. Not to get any baby food. And I told you, I wanted to be prepared. I don't know how long we'll have to take care of Toni."

"She won't be ready to eat that stuff for months," Grace snapped. "Are you planning on keeping her hidden away in here for that long? I think the police will have a thing or two to say about that."

A door across the hall opened. "Mr. Salvatore? What's going on out there? Who's using profanity?"

"Mrs. Bumgartle," Luc said, his smile less captivating than usual. He climbed over the spilled baby food jars. "Did we wake you? I'm so sorry."

To Grace's astonishment, Luc's unfailing charm failed. Utterly. It was, without question, a first. The old woman adjusted her glasses on the tip of her long, narrow nose and scowled. "Is that a baby?"

"Where?" He glanced over his shoulder. "Oh, that? Why, yes. That is a baby, isn't it?"

Mrs. Bumgartle's eyes narrowed. "I'm delighted we agree that it's a baby. The question is, whose baby is it?"

"Whose baby...?"

"Yes, Mr. Salvatore." She yanked the belt of her thick woolen robe tight about her ample middle. "Whose baby do you have there?"

"It's my brother's baby," Luc explained. "This is my niece. We're baby-sitting her for a short time."

"Just baby-sitting," Grace confirmed. "That's all we're doing."

Mrs. Bumgartle looked from Luc to Grace, her gaze finally settling with needlepoint sharpness on Luc. "You, Mr. Salvatore, are up to something," she said in clear, carrying tones. "And I suspect it's nothing good." With that she disappeared back into her apartment.

Luc sighed in exasperation. "Great. Just great. Open the door, Grace, and let's get out of the hallway before we wake up the entire apartment complex."

"Here." Passing him the baby, Grace applied herself to the unyielding lock with due diligence. A moment later the door swung inward.

Grace held out her arms for Toni and stepped into Luc's apartment, fumbling for the light. Luc picked up the numerous bags of groceries and baby paraphernalia, kicked the spilled jars of baby food in the general direction of the entranceway and followed her in. He fought to close the door.

"You've left half the jars outside," she informed him.

"Since you're so certain we don't need any baby food, they can stay out there until I'm good and ready to go after them." His jaw inched out and he leaned down until his nose almost touched hers. "You have a problem with that?"

"Not I," she was quick to assure him. "Mrs. Bumgartle might, however."

"You leave Mrs. Bumgartle to me," he said, dropping his armload to the floor of the front hall. "I'll talk to her."

A tiny, unladylike snort escaped. "Charm her you mean, like you do every other woman in the world? Or perhaps the operative word is *lie*."

Luc merely glanced at her, then dug through their purchases until he uncovered the portable crib. It took him less than a minute to open it and settle Toni inside. He carried the baby into the living room, and there faced Grace. "For your information, Miss Barnes, I never lie."

"Oh, really? What do you call that story you told the police?"

"A truth-to-be," came the prompt reply. "Because the truth is we are baby-sitting my niece. And the truth is Pietro and Carina will return for Toni. And the truth is they will soon be married or suffer the consequences."

"What about our so-called engagement?"

He shook his head. "I think we'll save that particular truth for a future discussion. I'm not proud of what I did today. But I considered it imperative. I hate lying and I hate liars...." He seemed to watch her closely. "Which is why I get along so well with you, Grace."

A blush lit her face and she prayed he would attribute it to embarrassment rather than sudden, intense guilt. Because if he ever found out about her conspiracy with Dom, Luc would be very angry. It would also change everything between them, and she realized for the first time how much she'd hate that change. "Luc—"

"As far as charming women," he interrupted ruthlessly, "of course I'm charming to women. I told you. I love women. I adore women. They're easy to be charming to. What's wrong with that?"

She took a hasty step back. "Noth-nothing."

He swallowed the distance between them in one stride. "If," he continued, his voice dipping low and taking on a raspy edge, "you weren't so cold and remote, I'd have been more charming to you, too. Only that and one other thing has held me back these past eleven months."

Grace swallowed nervously. "What's the one other thing?" she dared to ask.

"Your engagement," he responded promptly. "And do you know why?"

"No," she whispered.

He leaned forward, his eyes gleaming gold in the subdued lighting. "Because I don't poach." He took another step toward her and smiled, a predatory sort of smile. "Until now." And then he reached for her.

"No!" Grace shook her head frantically, pushing her hands against his chest. "You're only saying that to... to..."

Luc tilted his head to one side. "To what?"

To drive me crazy. To tempt me beyond endurance. "To... to give me a hard time," she insisted, leaping at the only safe excuse she could think of. "But it's not true. Maybe if I were beautiful like your other women—"

He cut through her words without hesitation. "All women are beautiful. Even women who hide behind these." He slipped off her glasses, dangling them carelessly from one finger.

"I need those!" She made a grab for the glasses, but he tossed them aside with casual disregard. They hit the soft cushions of the couch, bounced once and settled in the middle of the cushions, the lenses winking in the subdued lighting.

"You need them?" he asked and she couldn't mistake the irony in his voice.

Did he know? Did he suspect the glasses were part of her disguise? She didn't dare lie. Not when he watched her so closely. Not when she felt so vulnerable, stripped of the defenses she'd worked so long and hard to maintain between them. Instead, she fought his hold. "Luc, stop it!"

He didn't listen. Nor did he release her. "What I don't understand is why." His fingers slid into her hair, scattering the pins, the heavy curls tumbling free. "Why would a woman as beautiful as you..."

"No, don't!" She tried to step back, but he cupped her shoulders and refused to let go. To her horror, his hands drifted downward, gently tracing the curves hidden by her voluminous blouse and thick woolen skirt, before settling on her hips.

"...want to hide her light beneath a bushel?" he finished in satisfaction. "And you have been hiding your light, haven't you, my sweet? Is that Will-William's doing, I wonder?"

"Luc, please," she moaned, struggling to slip free.

He tightened his hold on her hips, yanking her closer. "You, *cara mia,* are stunning," he whispered, his mouth a hairbreadth away. "And for just this once, good old Will-William can go to hell."

CHAPTER FOUR

The Great Lie
Day 337 at 23 hours, 29 minutes...

LUC DIDN'T TRY to force a kiss on her as Grace half expected...half hoped. Instead his fingers combed through her loosened hair and he cupped her head, the rough edges of his thumb stroking a line of fire along her jaw. He bent closer, his rich golden eyes glowing with a fire and passion that trapped her, entangled her in a web of long-suppressed need and desire.

A small, still rational part of her knew she shouldn't be allowing this to happen. She should be resisting, fighting his touch...his hold...his charm. She was supposed to be an engaged woman, for heaven's sake. She couldn't allow Luc to believe she could be so easily seduced by a man other than her fiancé.

As though reading her mind, he brushed a swift, gentle kiss across her lips. "Forget William. This has nothing to do with him. This is between the two of us, something that we've both been curious about for a long time."

She shook her head. "That's not true," she instantly denied.

"No?" His expression mocked her. "You've never thought about how it would feel to be held in my arms?"

"Never," she affirmed.

"You've never wondered how my kisses compare to William's?"

"I'm perfectly satisfied with my fiancé," she insisted, adding for good measure, "in every way."

He continued to hold her, his hands tangled in her hair, his thumb teasing along her jaw to the tiny pearl stud centered in her earlobe. "You're trembling."

"I'm cold."

"No, you're warm. And soft. And your cheeks…" He stroked the ridge of her cheekbone with his fingertip. "They're flushed with desire."

"That's makeup, not desire."

"You aren't wearing any makeup. At least, not blush." His voice dropped, seducing her with its deep, lilting timbre. "And what about your eyes? They're the most beautiful shade of green I've ever seen. But they give you away. They're glowing."

"They aren't glowing. They're glazed because I can't see without my glasses."

He laughed in genuine amusement, his smile a gleaming flash in his bronzed face. "You, Grace Barnes, are having a serious problem with fibs today. That'll have to stop—and I know just how to make sure it does."

She knew what he intended. He was going to kiss her. And when he did, she wouldn't have the strength to resist. "Luc, don't," she pleaded, attempting one last time to prevent the inevitable. "You'll regret it. We'll both regret it."

He shrugged, his smile fading, his expression turning serious. "You may be right, but at least let me give us something worthy of regret." His thumb drifted across her lower lip, teasing the fullness of her mouth for an instant before he lowered his head and finally kissed her.

It was magic. The instant his lips touched hers, her heartbeat doubled. She couldn't get enough, every sense throbbing to life, the blood singing through her veins. She could smell his distinctive spicy scent, feel the hard planes and angles of his body beneath her hands, hear the sound of his harsh breathing whispering in her ears. Even the taste of him intoxicated her, the sweet, delicious flavor driving all reason from her mind and leaving in its place pure sensation.

His hand slid down her spine, his arm wrapping around her waist and pulling her up against him. She fit perfectly. But somehow she'd always suspected she would. Unable to help herself, she wound her arms around his neck and returned his kiss.

It had been a long time since she'd last been in a man's arms. Too long. She'd forgotten how wonderful it could be. Yet this was different ... and the difference unsettled her. There was a peculiar combination of finding both sanctuary and jeopardy within Luc's arms, of knowing both security and vulnerability. He was at once a delight and a threat. Worst of all, he was a temptation—a temptation she couldn't afford to indulge in.

As though sensing her alarm, Toni began to cry. It was a timely interruption. Grace pulled free of Luc's arms and knelt beside the portable crib. Scooping up the baby, she turned to face the picture windows, her back to Luc.

She could see his image mirrored in the plate glass. His hands balled into fists, his chest rising and falling with each ragged breath. So ... she hadn't been the only one affected. That knowledge didn't bring her any relief. Instead, her alarm grew. The path they walked led to disaster, and she had too much at stake to follow blindly along. She had to end this before it went any further.

"I'll change Toni and then it's time I went home," she announced in a calm, unemotional voice.

"Feel free to change her," Luc agreed, coming up behind and dropping his hands to her shoulders. "But you aren't going anywhere. Not tonight and not tomorrow night, either."

She didn't dare turn around. She knew from long experience what that tone meant, heard the determination and the intensity that roughened his voice. She'd never yet won an argument when he spoke like that. Still, she had to try.

"You can handle Toni on your own. You don't need me. I'll return first thing in the morning—"

His hands tightened and he forced her to face him. "No. You promised to stay until Pietro or Carina returned, and I intend to hold you to that promise."

She'd also promised his father she wouldn't become personally involved with Luc. Seemed her promises weren't worth a plugged nickel these days. "Luc... It isn't right that I stay. It's not—"

"Proper?" He laughed, the sound harsh and empty of humor. "Do you think I give a damn about what's proper? I care about that baby you're holding. I care about doing what's best for her. What I know about infants can be summed up in one word. *Niente.* Nothing."

She frowned. "I don't know much more than you. Besides, you've learned the essentials today. You know how to change her, how to feed her. Surely you can get through one night without me."

A strange look glittered in his eyes. "I might. But why should I? I want you here, right beside me, helping to make sensible decisions."

"Hire a professional nanny," she suggested in desperation.

He shook his head. "Too risky. I don't want to chance the police becoming involved again. It's only for another day or two. Soon Pietro and Carina will return for Toni and everything will be back to normal."

Grace cuddled Toni close, inhaling the sweet aroma of powder and formula and baby. Things would never return to normal. Her life had been irreversibly altered. She could only hope it would all work out in the end. That Pietro and Carina would return. That Toni would be reunited with her parents. That Luc could be held at a safe distance. And that Dom would never learn of her brief indiscretion.

But most of all she hoped she could escape with a whole heart, that her brush with insanity wouldn't have any lasting repercussions. Because she knew that when it came to women, Luc couldn't be trusted. Besides, she had a dream to fulfill, a promise to keep. She wouldn't allow Luc or anyone else to distract her from her goal.

"I won't touch you again tonight," Luc said unexpectedly. "You'll be safe here with me. I swear it."

Safe? Not likely. She glanced down at Toni and her shoulders sagged. She really didn't have any choice, she realized. If she hadn't been able to abandon the baby earlier, she certainly couldn't do it now. What she could do was make sure that she didn't share any further intimacies with Luc. She'd hold him at a distance. She could do it. She'd had more than eleven months of practice accomplishing precisely that. The few weeks left would be a cinch.

"All right, I'll stay," she agreed.

Satisfaction glittered in his eyes. "You can sleep in one of my shirts. And I'll bring you a spare robe and a toothbrush. There are only two bedrooms. Do you want the baby tonight or should I take her in with me?"

"I'll care for her tonight, and you can have tomorrow," she said, her reply conceding that there would be a tomorrow night.

He nodded. "Fine. There's a bathroom that adjoins the guest bedroom. If you'd like to grab a shower, I'll watch the little stinker."

"Stinker?" A tiny smile escaped before she could prevent it. "Diapers are in the hall."

With that, she headed for the bathroom. In minutes she stood beneath a hot, relaxing deluge, rinsing away the tension of an unbelievably stressful day. Wishing she could stand there forever, she squared her shoulders, took a deep breath and reluctantly turned the shower off. Returning to the bedroom, she found a silk shirt and robe spread out on the bed.

Dressing quickly, she brushed her wet hair. She'd have to get another bottle of color rinse and soon. Already she could see the natural gold gleaming through the muddy brown dye. Another shampoo or two and this part of her disguise would be uncovered, as well. And what would Luc say then?

She shuddered. It didn't bear contemplation.

A soft knock sounded on the door. "You decent?" Luc called. At her affirmative response, he came in carrying Toni. "I've changed her and offered a bottle. She didn't seem very interested. If you'll take her, I'll bring in the portable crib."

In short order, he had them settled for the night. Grace stood in the middle of the room, uncomfortable beneath Luc's watchful eye. From the expression on his face she was fairly certain her disguise was shot to pieces. Not that it hadn't been when he kissed her...touched her. He had to have realized that she wore clothing several sizes too big. Standing before him now, wearing nothing but a clingy shirt and a silk paisley robe, there must be no doubt in his mind.

"Is there anything else you need?" he asked softly.

She shook her head, the damp curls swirling about her neck and shoulders. "Nothing, thanks. I'll...I'll see you in the morning."

"No question about it. But if you do need any-thing—" He grinned. "Anything at all, don't hesitate to come and get me."

She lifted her chin and gave him a cool look. "I can cope."

"Goodnight, then." He started to close the door, then stuck his head back in. "Oh, and Grace?"

She stared at him warily. "Yes?"

"I notice you seem to see just fine without those glasses. A miracle cure, perhaps?"

The door banged closed behind him and Grace let out a small groan of despair. How could she have been so foolish? And what must he be thinking? Perhaps she could tell him her eyes were sensitive to light. Perhaps she could say that the doctor prescribed tinted glasses to prevent eyestrain.

She sighed. Perhaps she should dispense with all the lies and hope something could be salvaged from this mess. She glanced over at Toni. The baby slept soundly, her rounded bottom thrust high in the air, a chubby fist pressed against her puckered mouth. Tucking the blanket securely around her tiny form, Grace crossed to her own bed, slipped beneath the covers and turned off the bedside lamp.

Moonlight brightened the room and she folded her arms behind her head, studying the ceiling. Here she was, bedding down for the night in Luc's apartment. If Dom ever found out, he'd have a coronary. She yawned. She'd just have to make sure that he never did.

More important, she'd have to make sure that Luc never found out she wasn't really engaged. Somehow, she suspected that if he did she'd find herself in deep, deep trouble. And not just for having lied to him. That kiss had been a mistake. A big mistake. A mistake she had no intention of ever repeating.

Four more weeks to get through.

All of a sudden, it seemed a lifetime.

A THUMP SOUNDED SOMEWHERE deep in the apartment and Grace rolled over, glaring at the clock on the night-stand. It couldn't be three in the morning. It couldn't be. She hadn't slept a wink. This was all Luc's fault. He had to have the noisiest apartment in the entire complex. Every little sound made her jump. Worse, it made Toni jump. Whenever the baby had been on the verge of drifting off, some tiny noise would wake her and she'd start to fuss.

Right on cue, a pitiful wail rose from the far side of the room and Grace groaned. Struggling out of bed, she shoved a tumble of curls from her eyes and approached the crib.

"I'm coming, munchkin," she muttered. "Keep your diapers on." Toni lay on her back, her covers kicked off, her feet pumping like a crazed locomotive. Two chubby fists pinwheeled the air. Grace eyed the activity with deep suspicion. "You do that to help suck in more air, don't you?" she asked the red-faced infant. "And once you're finished inhaling, out it all comes in one huge bellow. Right?"

Not giving Toni time to vent her agreement, Grace picked up the baby and slipped from the room. Where had Luc left the diapers and bottles? To her relief, the diapers were in plain sight in the living room. She found bottles of formula already mixed in the refrigerator. A short spin in the microwave warmed the milk to the perfect temperature.

Returning to the living room, Grace drew a chair over to the picture window and settled into it, Toni nestled in the crook of her arm. San Francisco glittered before her. Even at three in the morning, the city seemed alive with lights and movement.

A nearly full moon hung in the sky, the light spilling through the window, bathing the room in its silver glow. Grace stared down at Toni. With her flushed olive skin and huge dark eyes, she was the most adorable creature Grace had ever seen. How could Carina bear to be separated from this precious bundle for even one tiny moment? It must have been pure agony for her to make such a decision.

And what about being twenty, a foreign-exchange student and an unwed mother? In all likelihood, poor Carina hadn't dared go home to face her parents with the results of her indiscretion. She'd apparently been just as reluctant to turn to Pietro for help, though the reason for that wasn't quite as clear. Of course, if Pietro was half the womanizer Luc was, Grace could understand Carina's reluctance. And yet...

Grace frowned. Somehow, she couldn't see Luc abandoning his lover in her time of need, let alone his child. Nor could she imagine him leaving any woman in the lurch—he cared about them too deeply. Unfortunately, he cared too deeply about all women to ever settle on any one. Still...

She knew Luc. He would have done everything in his power to prevent an accident like Pietro and Carina's from occurring in the first place. But if it had, he would have taken on the responsibility of both mother and child. She didn't doubt that for one minute. And wasn't that just what Pietro was attempting to do? Perhaps it was a Salvatore trait.

Grace gazed down at the baby in her arms, filled with an overwhelming desire to protect this child. She could fully understand Luc's determination to keep Toni safe. In less than twenty-four hours, she'd grown impossibly attached to Toni, herself. She could even imagine having a baby like this one. She could imagine the father, too.

There was just one catch. She wanted a man who would love her exclusively, who'd choose her above all other women and never once look back. She bit down on her lip, tears stinging her eyes. That man wouldn't be Luc. Not a chance. She stared out the window, and suddenly her reflection was joined by another and Luc crossed to her side.

"Everything all right?" he asked in a soft voice, stooping beside the chair.

"Everything's fine." She bowed her head, embarrassed to be caught with tears in her eyes. She hadn't realized how much she depended on her tinted glasses to conceal her thoughts and emotions from him. Come morning, those glasses would once again be perched on the end of her nose. "Toni woke up hungry and wet."

Luc's mouth curved into a wry smile. "Even with only a single day's experience of baby care, I've discovered they have a nasty tendency to do that." He eyed Grace closely. "You look tired. Want me to take over for a while?"

Her throat tightened and she shook her head. "I'm fine," she managed to say. He reached out and tucked a curl behind her ear, his touch unexpectedly gentle and soothing.

"You don't sound fine. You sound exhausted." His hand moved from her hair to her shoulder, massaging the tense muscles along the back of her neck. "It's going to work out, Grace. I know everything looks a bit bleak now—"

"What if she doesn't come back?" The question practically burst from Grace. "What if she abandons Toni?"

He didn't hesitate for an instant. "Then Pietro will take care of his daughter. And we'll work it out somehow." He seemed so strong, so resolute. "This baby's a Salvatore. And I'll do everything within my power to protect her."

She didn't doubt him. "Your family's lucky to have you to watch out for them," she told Luc quietly.

"And your fiancé's lucky to have you. Not many women would have done what you did today."

A tiny smile touched her mouth and she glanced at him. "Was there a choice?"

He didn't return her smile. Instead his gaze was filled with an intensity that unnerved her. "Yes. You had a choice. You could have walked. You could have told me to go to hell. But you didn't. You stuck by me, Grace. That means a lot."

His thick, dark hair tumbled across his brow and a shadow of stubble clung to his jaw. He'd thrown on a robe not unlike the one he'd loaned her, and she suspected he wore little or nothing beneath it. The robe veed deeply and she could see the crisp, dark hair covering his chest. For a crazy instant she almost reached out and touched him.

She closed her eyes. It was late. She was tired. And he attracted her more than any man she'd ever known. "Luc, you have to leave now," she whispered.

Turning to him, she saw the passion spark to life in his eyes, saw the hint of a flush mount his angled cheekbones. "You look very beautiful sitting in the moonlight," he murmured. "It streaks your hair with shiny gold threads."

She froze. "A trick of the light," she insisted. "Go to bed, Luc. Please. You promised."

"I promised I wouldn't kiss you again last night. But I didn't make any promises about today. And in case you hadn't noticed, this is a brand-new day. Nor did I promise I wouldn't sit in the moonlight with you. That I wouldn't talk to you. That I wouldn't watch you hold Toni as if she were your own."

His every word seduced her. She turned her head away, turned from near overwhelming temptation. "You're forgetting about my fiancé."

"No, I'm not. But perhaps you should forget about him. He isn't good enough for you. Not if he encourages you to wear those ridiculous outfits and scrape your hair back instead of leaving it loose around your face. You're so beautiful, Grace. And hiding that beauty is a sin."

The bottle empty, Grace lifted Toni to her shoulder and patted the infant's back, using this moment to gather the remaining shreds of her composure. At last she forced herself to say, "Luc, I'm your assistant. I'm engaged to be married. You asked for my help and I'm helping you. Don't make this more difficult than necessary. I'm not interested in having a . . . a relationship with you. I have William." For the first time she got that name out without stammering. "He's all I need. All I'll ever need."

She might as well have struck Luc. He reared back, and without another word he stood and walked away. For an insane instant, Grace considered following him, confessing the truth. But she knew she couldn't. She couldn't afford to become emotionally involved with Luc. Not if she wanted her own business. And not if she wanted to come out of this situation with her heart intact.

"RISE AND SHINE!" Grace rolled over and groaned, flinging an arm across her face to block out the blinding sunlight. "Go away," she snarled.

Luc chuckled. "I have coffee," he tempted.

She peeked out from beneath her elbow. "Coffee?"

"A cup for now and a whole fresh-brewed pot waiting in the kitchen."

She sat up and looked over at the crib. It was empty. "Where's Toni?"

"On a blanket in the living room shaking her fist at dust motes." He headed for the door. "We have a lot to do today, so hurry up and get dressed."

Drawing her knees to her chest, she said, "I don't have anything clean to wear."

"We'll stop by your apartment on the way to the stores. You can change and pack a few days' worth of clothes."

She eyed him suspiciously. "A few days?"

"A few days," he confirmed. "Pietro called." And with that he breezed from the room.

It took ten minutes to pull herself together. The coffee helped substantially. After locating her glasses on the living room couch and popping them on the end of her nose, she swept the carpet for her scattered hairpins and pocketed them. Reluctant to face reality—even more reluctant to hear what Pietro had to say when he'd called, she played with Toni for a while. Eventually, hunger forced her to track Luc down in the kitchen. Open confrontation seemed the best course of action.

"What do you mean a few days?" she demanded, jumping right in. "What did Pietro say?"

"He missed connecting with Carina in Italy. Her mother is being seen by a specialist in Switzerland, and Carina went there. Pietro's following."

"Did you tell him about the police? Did you tell him we haven't a clue how to take care of a baby? When's he coming back?"

"Yes. Yes. And as soon as possible." Luc ran a hand through his hair, an edge of impatience creeping into his voice. "You're upset about this, and so am I. But there isn't anything I can do about it. Not yet. So let's make the best of things."

Right. Until the police showed up. Or worse, Dom. And then Luc's clever, little scheme would come crashing down around both their ears. And so would Dom's... She tried to stay calm. Shrieking wouldn't accomplish a thing. Except make her feel a whole heck of a lot better. She took a deep breath, wavering between anger and capitulation. "What's your plan of action?" she finally asked, giving in to the inevitable. At least, with Luc, it was the inevitable.

"First we go to your apartment. Then we go shopping for Toni. I've called in at the office and had everything postponed for a few days. In the meantime..." He brandished the coffeepot. "Let me pour you more coffee. There's cereal for breakfast or I can scramble you some eggs."

"Cereal," she informed him coolly. "I can't face anything yellow first thing in the morning."

Once they'd eaten, they began to prepare for their outing. Getting ready to leave took longer than Grace ever could have thought possible. Packing the diaper bag alone was a major undertaking. "Diapers. Check. Wipes. Check. Powder. Check. Spare clothes. Check. More diapers. Double check."

"You forgot the bottles and formula."

She glared at Luc in exasperation. "Then you better get a second diaper bag, because nothing else will fit in here."

"How about a cooler for the formula?"

"Terrific. One more thing to carry. And how are we supposed to heat the bottles?"

"In a microwave, of course."

Keeping her temper while working for Luc, day after day, had proved a challenge. Keeping her temper while stuck with him day in and day out was an impossibility. She planted her hands on her hips. "A microwave? Were you planning on bringing that along with us, too?"

"That won't be necessary. Everyone has microwaves. We'll just ask to borrow somebody's." He slung the diaper bag over one shoulder, picked up the cooler and his jacket and headed for the door. "Come on, Grace. It's getting late and we have a lot to do today."

She folded her arms across her chest. "Aren't you forgetting something?"

He glanced around. "Diaper bag, cooler, jacket, changing pad and a garbage bag for dirty diapers. Nope. Got it all."

Grace sighed. "Everything except the baby. Why don't I take care of that?"

Thirty minutes later, they'd crossed the Bay Bridge out of San Francisco and reached the small apartment Grace rented on the Oakland-Berkeley line. A short walk from

BART, the electric railway, it was an easy commute to work each day and much less expensive than living in the city.

"I'll just run upstairs and pack a bag," she suggested. "Why don't you wait here with Toni."

To her dismay Luc released his seat belt, climbed out of the car and calmly unfastened the baby from her car seat. "Toni would like to see your apartment and so would I. Besides, I want to make sure you don't pack any of William's clothes."

She stared at him in confusion. "William's clothes?"

"Two sizes too large and three decades too old."

Having no choice, she led the way to her door. "Make yourself at home," she said with more than a hint of irony. "I'll go pack."

In the bedroom, she yanked a small cloth suitcase down from the shelf in her closet and began tossing in the essentials. A minute later, Luc and Toni appeared at the door.

And in Luc's hand was her third-place award for Salvatore's young-entrepreneur contest.

He held it up, his eyes cool and watchful. "What's this, Grace?"

CHAPTER FIVE

The Great Lie
Day 338 and Grace's disguise is slipping...

CROSSING TO LUC'S side, Grace took the award from him and placed it on her bureau. "You know what it is."

"You're right, I do. I guess my question is, what are you doing with it?"

Returning to her packing, she carefully folded a blouse and tucked it into the suitcase. "I think that's obvious, too. I won it."

"In this past year's contest?"

"Why the questions, Luc?" she snapped. "What's the problem? Yes. I won third place in this past year's contest. As a result, I met Dom."

"And?"

"And," she finished impatiently, "he thought highly enough of me to recommend me for the job as your assistant. I thought you knew all that."

"No. I didn't."

He frowned, his gaze searching, and she glanced hastily away. But it was too late. He suspected she was hiding something, and knowing Luc he wouldn't leave it alone until he'd settled the issue to his satisfaction. She could practically see the wheels turning as he mulled over what he perceived to be a puzzle.

"Let's try this tack and see if it gets us anywhere . . ." he began. "*Why* did you take the job as my assistant?"

"This is ridiculous. I took the job for the same reason millions of people all over the world take jobs." Using less than her usual care, she balled up another blouse and thrust it into the suitcase. She just wanted to end this conversation and get out of here before she did something . . . said something . . . incriminating. "I needed to earn money."

"Yes, but contestants who enter the young-entrepreneur contest are interested in starting their own business, not working for someone else."

"What's your point, Luc?" There was an edge to her voice.

His eyes narrowed. "Are you? Interested in starting your own business?"

She couldn't lie. She'd told him enough of those already without making it any worse. Looking directly at him, she said, "Yes. I'm interested in *someday* starting my own business. In the meantime, working for you should be good experience."

He settled Toni in the crook of his arm and propped a shoulder against the doorjamb. "And has it been? Has working for me been good?"

She turned back to her packing. They continued to tread on dangerous ground—different ground, perhaps, but dangerous, nonetheless. "Yes. It's been good," she agreed shortly. In fact, it had been more than good. Working for Luc had been surprisingly enjoyable. She'd thrived on the challenges, appreciated the fast pace. She'd even relished their heated arguments. She frowned. She'd miss all that when she left.

"What sort of business do you plan to open?" he asked.

She glanced hesitantly at him. Would he laugh when she told him? "It'll be a toy store. One that specializes in babies. All the toys will be unique—handcrafted by local artisans, educational and safe." Her mother had always insisted on that.

He glanced down at Toni, a smile curving the corner of his mouth. "Seems we picked the perfect woman to help us, after all." He approached, his movements lithe and graceful. "Here. Take the kid."

She obeyed without thought. Not until he turned and began to rummage through her suitcase, did she realize his motives for handing her the baby. "Cut that out, Luc! You have no right going through my things."

"I just want to make sure what you pack is practical." He yanked out the skirt and blouse she'd just shoved in. "Which this is not," he decided, and reached for the next garment. "Nor is this."

"Stop that! Those are eminently practical and you know it."

"Practical for the office, not for taking care of a baby." He glanced at a skirt label. "This has to be dry-cleaned. One good burp and it's history."

"Luc!" Toni's little face screwed into a frown and Grace quickly moderated her tone to reflect sweetness and light. "Let me put it this way. You take one more item out of my suitcase, and I'll kill you." Too bad her glasses hid the glare she shot in his direction—not that he was looking anyway.

"As long as we're dispensing with the impractical, I think we'll dispense with the ugly, as well," he said, ignoring her threat. Clothes flew through the air and landed on the bed. "Ugly. Impractical. Ugly. Ugly. And very ugly. Don't you get depressed wearing this stuff?"

"No, I don't." At least, not often. Dom's promised reward offered more than adequate compensation. She scowled in impotent fury. "And what difference does it make if they're ugly? They don't belong to you."

He glanced up, a dangerous glitter in his golden eyes. "They may not belong to me, but I have to look at them. And so does Toni. I won't have you around my niece day and night, displaying such a lack of fashion taste. It'll warp her. Hell, it's already warped me."

"That's ridiculous!"

"Want to bet?" he asked derisively. "It's gotten so bad, I've begun to think brown is pretty. At least on you." Finished with the suitcase, he headed for her closet.

She looked about, desperate for a safe place to deposit the baby so she could stop him—physically, if necessary. "What are you doing now? Get out of there!"

"Hello. What's this?" He yanked free a mint green dress. "Ah, much better. Do you save this for when William's here...?" He lifted an eyebrow, his expression turning wicked. "Or perhaps it's to wear when William isn't around."

"William loves that dress!" she protested, then blinked. What the dickens was she saying?

"Sure he does. That's why he has you running about looking like a bag lady most of the time. That's one sick relationship you have going there."

"My relationship with Will...William is none of your concern." How she wished she could get that name past her lips without stammering. Unfortunately, nine times out of ten it wouldn't come.

"Your relationship with him isn't my concern...yet. But, give it time."

Grace stared in alarm. What did he mean? That at some point her relationship with William would become his concern? And precisely what did he have in mind, once it did? Confronting the nonexistent William? A tightness settled in her chest. Matters grew more complicated by the minute.

Rummaging through what she privately referred to as her off-duty clothing, he stripped a pair of soft rose-colored slacks, black stretch pants and several brightly patterned pullover sweaters from their hangers and dropped them into her suitcase. After a moment's consideration, he added a totally impractical white slip dress with a bolero jacket to the pile.

"What's that for?" she demanded.

"For the hell of it."

Clearly, nothing she could say would stop him. She hugged Toni to her breast. "Are you quite through?"

"No. Where are your cosmetics?" He crossed to her dresser. "Never mind. I've found them."

"I can do that," she insisted.

His response sounded suspiciously like a snort. He rifled through the bottles and tubes cluttering the tabletop with a knowledge and decisiveness that could only have come from long experience—a fact that didn't escape her. Clearly, he was familiar with women. With everything about women. But then, she'd long suspected that when it came to the fairer sex, Luc was an expert.

"Fascinating colors here," he said in disgust. "Not one of them suits you. Except... Here we go." He swept foundation, blush, eye shadow, mascara and lipstick into a cosmetic bag and tossed it into her suitcase. Then he turned and folded his arms across his chest. "What's going on, Grace?"

She shoved her glasses high up on the bridge of her nose and cuddled Toni close, as if for protection. "I don't know what you're talking about," she claimed. But they both knew she lied.

He lifted an eyebrow, his expression sardonic. "Oh, no? Two separate wardrobes. Two distinct sets of cosmetics. And you have no comment?"

"Right. I have no comment."

The dangerous light reappeared in his eyes. "You have no comment... yet."

She swallowed. There was that word again. "Yet?"

He crossed to stand directly in front of her. "Yet. It implies a temporary situation." He leaned down until they were almost nose to nose. "One that *will* change in the near future. Are we clear on that?"

She took a hasty step backward. "Crystal."

"Fine." He turned to her suitcase and zipped the bag closed. "Just so you know, I'm taking this new Grace home with me. I've had the other at the office for quite long enough." He lifted the suitcase off the bed and eased Toni from her arms. "Get changed and meet me down at the car. Next stop—Toys-a-Trillion."

She didn't dare say another word. He was letting her off easy and she knew it. She also didn't doubt for one little minute that he'd eventually ask some pointed questions. She nibbled her lower lip. What would she say when he demanded answers? The thought of telling him the truth about her "deal" with Dom appalled her.

It had all seemed so simple and harmless when the idea had first been proposed. But now... Luc would not react well if he found out. And the chances of his uncovering the truth were becoming more and more likely. Which made her dream of starting her own business more and more *un*likely.

She didn't waste any time. Stripping off her dirty clothes, she rushed through her shower. Next came a hasty debate over whether to wear off-duty clothes or office clothing. Wrapped in a wet towel, she stood shivering in front of her closet considering her choices—not that her decision took a lot of thought. Office won, hands down. Whether it was a perverse gesture on her part or a desperate need to cling to what camouflage she could, Grace couldn't say. But the bulky wool suit in a nondescript shade of gray gave her back a sense of security she hadn't experienced since Toni had fallen into their lives. Gathering up a fistful of pins, she slicked back her damp hair and skewered the wayward curls into a tight, forbidding knot at the nape of her neck. She still hadn't acquired any more dye, nor did she have any extra bottles stashed at the apartment. Already bright gold streaks could be detected beneath the mousy brown rinse. How long would it be before Luc noticed—assuming he hadn't already?

Disguise somewhat in place, she left her apartment. Joining Luc in the car, she glanced anxiously at him to see how he reacted to her costume. Aside from sparing her a quick glance of amusement, he didn't say a word. Instead, he put the car in motion.

It took them another half hour to drive to the toy store. Located in the East Bay near a mall, the huge barn of a building contained every imaginable toy ever invented. Grace looked around in bewilderment. She'd never seen so many toys. And the setup! Some insane person had stacked the inventory from the floor to the thirty-foot ceiling. How in the world could anyone possibly obtain, let alone purchase the higher-altitude items? Crazed kids raced up and down the aisles scrambling through the displays, harried mothers in hot pursuit. One ambitious youngster busily climbed the shelving above her head.

She turned to Luc. "Get the manager before that child kills himself," she ordered.

Luc simply grinned. "Be glad it isn't closer to Christmas. This place turns into a real zoo, then."

"You've been here before?" she asked in astonishment.

"Of course. Haven't you?"

"No," she admitted, eyeing the determined climber. "And if I'm very lucky, I never will again."

"Don't be such a spoilsport." He reached above her, plucked the squirming youngster off the shelf and set him on the floor. Hollering in protest, the boy rounded a corner and disappeared from view. "I do all my Christmas shopping here. My brothers count on it."

"Your brothers are grown men," she informed him.

"Yes, but they're kids at heart. And they like toys." He grabbed a cart. "Let's get down to business. Follow me."

"Where are you going?" Without answering, he headed toward the middle of the store. Grace scurried behind. She'd be lost in here for the next five months, if she didn't keep up with him.

Presently he stopped in the infant department. "Take a look at these. Baby pouches." Without further ado, he ripped a carton apart, removed the pouch and tossed the empty box in the shopping basket. "Let's try it on for size."

"Luc!" she exclaimed, appalled. "You can't do that. They'll arrest you for shoplifting or something."

He shot her a look of disapproval. "Shoplifting implies leaving without paying for something. I would never do such a thing. The box is in my cart, plain as day. And

I have an eager little plastic gold card revving in my pocket."

"But—"

"Relax, Gracie. They know me here." He frowned at the sling, examining it from various angles. "How the hell does this thing work?"

"Maybe if we read the directions?" she suggested.

"Directions are for amateurs."

"We *are* amateurs," she reminded gently. She picked up the box. "It looks like you fasten the two top straps around your neck and the bottom two around your waist."

"I know that! But it doesn't show which is the top and which is the bottom. Wait a sec... Got it." He fastened the belts and snaps and grinned, spreading his arms wide. "What do you think? Is Toni ready for her first ride?"

Grace bit her lip to keep from smiling. "No."

He frowned. "No?"

"You put her in there the way it is now and you'll dump your precious niece right on her cute little head."

He peered down at the pouch. Sure enough, the opening for the head pointed south, the leg holes pointed north. "Well, shoot," he muttered, nonplussed.

A salesgirl appeared at his elbow, white teeth flashing, lashes fluttering. She flipped her long bleached hair over one shoulder and planted a hand on her trim hip. Her name tag read, "Hi! Debbi can't wait to assist you!"

"Why, Mr. Salvatore," Debbi-who-couldn't-wait-to-assist squealed. At least it sounded like a squeal to Grace... a squeal reminiscent of those emitted by the porcine family. "You haven't visited for ages. Is there something I can help you with?"

He gestured at the baby sling strapped to his chest. "What am I doing wrong?" he asked with a helpless,

men-are-all-thumbs-when-it-comes-to-baby-contraptions
grin.

"You put it on upside down," Grace pointed out
acerbically.

Debbi pursed her lips. "I think you put it on upside
down," she proclaimed, as if she'd just invented the
thought.

Removing the sling, she flipped it around and then re-
fastened it. In the process her hands managed to investigate every square inch of Luc's torso. Clearly satisfied
with the results of her investigation and with the position of the sling, she gave the pouch a final pat.

Unable…or unwilling…to explain her reaction to dear
Debbi, Grace stepped forward the second the salesgirl
stepped back. But helping Luc slip Toni into the sling
while at the same time doing her level best to flash her
engagement ring under Debbi's nose proved to be a
challenge she couldn't resist. "That's perfect," she announced and even managed a friendly smile in the salesgirl's direction. "Antonia's the first Salvatore girl
in…how many generations, Luc?"

"A lot."

"The family's thrilled. Absolutely thrilled. Aren't they,
Luc?"

He lifted a quizzical eyebrow. "Oh, they're thrilled, all
right."

The salesgirl looked from Luc to Antonia to Grace to
Grace's ring and sighed. "How…how thrilling. Well, if
I can help you with anything else, don't hesitate to call."

"Oh, we will," Grace assured her. Yes, they'd definitely hesitate before calling. "Bye."

With a final, wistful glance in Luc's direction, Debbi
trotted down the aisle.

"Grace... Grace... Grace," Luc murmured, shaking his head, his golden eyes glittering with laughter. "What has happened to my cool, aloof assistant?"

She lifted her chin. "I haven't a clue what you're talking about." A long moment of silence stretched between them, and she could feel the hot color mount her cheeks. Desperate to escape his probing gaze, she made a pretence of checking to be sure Toni rested comfortably in the sling. Not that she fooled anyone. The baby, tucked close to Luc's heart, slept peacefully in her little pouch.

"What's next on the list?" Grace asked, unable to stand the strained silence for another instant.

"You."

Her eyes widened and she took a hasty step back. "Wh-what?"

He cupped her elbow in one hand and pushed the cart with his other. "All good temporary mothers need a stroller. So next we get you a stroller." He eyed her, a wicked grin curving his mouth. "What did you think I meant?"

She cleared her throat. "Why, precisely that, of course."

He released a gusty sigh. "I see you haven't used them all up."

She gave him a suspicious look. "Used up what?"

"Your quota of fibs."

With that, he headed toward the center of the store, where racks of strollers were displayed. He tried several models, pushing them about, cornering sharply to see if they tipped. He even pulled down a double stroller for inspection.

"We only have one baby," Grace pointed out.

"With all the junk she needs, we could use the other side for storage."

Actually, he had a point. "What about the one over here? It's dual purpose. You can hook the two strollers together to form a double or separate them into individual units."

"Sold." He removed a large box from the shelves and fitted it into the cart. "Now for the serious stuff." He grinned down at her. "Toys."

Two hours...and three carts later, Grace decided to call a halt to his shopping binge. "This is ridiculous, Luc. The baby can't use a tenth of what you're buying. It'll go to waste."

"Don't fuss," Luc replied, swooping up a dozen rattles. "Anything Carina and the baby can't use, I'll donate to charity. Relax and enjoy yourself. Spend some of my money. Better yet, spend a lot of my money. I'm having fun. Aren't you having fun?"

"Yes, but..."

"Then, not another word of argument." He leaned closer, his eyes dark and intent. "I'm tired of the 'office Grace,'" he murmured. "Send her home and let the other Grace come out and play. The one who wears pale green dresses that match her eyes and tight stretch pants with soft wool sweaters. I want to get to know that Grace."

She shook her head, suddenly afraid. She was out of her depth and knew it. All her lies were steadily unraveling and soon she'd be exposed and vulnerable. She didn't dare consider what might happen then....

To her relief, Toni chose that moment to put an end to both their conversation and the shopping spree. Finished with her nap, she began to complain bitterly and at great volume at being trapped for so long in the baby sling.

"Time for a bottle, young lady," Grace decreed, lifting her off Luc's chest. "If you'll let me have the diaper bag, Luc, I'll go feed and change Toni while you give your credit card a workout."

"I checked and there's a microwave in the employee lounge. They won't mind you heating up Toni's bottle there. I'll come and get you once I've loaded the car."

Grace glanced at the overflowing carts and grimaced. "Now I know why families buy those huge vans when they start having kids."

Luc snapped his fingers. "Vans. That's what I forgot to buy. Let's see... I think they're over on aisle eight next to the Lear jets."

"Very funny." Grace rocked the tearful Toni, gently patting her back. "We girls will be in the lounge with our feet up enjoying a warm mug of formula. See you in a while."

To her surprise, Luc joined them a few minutes later. Though why it should surprise her, she didn't know. She suspected the powers-that-be at Toys-a-Trillion tended to jump through hoops when Luc Salvatore walked into their store—especially if he was in the habit of spending as much as he had today. By the time she'd finished with Toni, the most important of their selections were paid for and loaded in the car, the rest to be delivered the next day. It amazed her what charm and money could accomplish.

Having fastened Toni into her car seat, Grace buckled her own seat belt and sighed. "I need to get back to work so I can rest," she joked.

"You can rest tonight. I've invited my brothers over for dinner, and you can relax while they entertain Toni."

She glanced over at him. "Do they know about her?"

He started the engine and pulled out of the parking space. "I thought I'd surprise them. That way I can impress on them the importance of keeping this information quiet until Pietro and Carina return."

"And do your brothers always fall in with your demands?"

He inclined his head. "They tend to find it in their best interest to do things my way."

"Because you're the oldest?"

He grinned. "That, and the fact that I'm their boss. He who controls the purse strings..."

"Calls the tune?"

"The metaphor may be mixed, but the meaning's accurate enough."

Accurate, indeed. She nibbled her lip. If she were smart, she'd do well to remember who called the tune she danced to... and who controlled the future purse strings for Baby Dream Toys.

"GRACE! That's the doorbell. Could you get it? I'm up to my elbows in... in... in real nasty stuff."

Crossing to the front hall, she opened the door. All four of Luc and Pietro's brothers stood grouped in the hallway arguing volubly. "Ten bucks, it's good news."

"Fifteen, it's bad."

"Twenty to one, he's gone and got himself engaged."

"Not Luc. Not a chance. I'll bet twenty-five dollars you're all wrong."

The door across the hall opened and Mrs. Bumgartle peered out. "What's going on there? Who's gambling?"

"Hello, Mrs. Bumgartle," the four chorused a greeting.

"Don't give me any of your lip," she retorted. "Gambling's illegal in this state, you know."

"It's just a friendly wager," Alessandro assured her. "Just trying to figure out what Luc's up to."

"He's up to no good. No good a'tall," she snapped. "Now, stop cluttering the hall, or I'll call the building manager." With that, the door banged closed.

Grace cleared her throat. "Would you gentlemen care to come in?"

"Oh, hello, Grace," Alessandro said, leading the way into the apartment. "Something special going on?"

"No cheating!" the twins, Marc and Stef, exclaimed in unison.

"And no fair pumping Grace," Rocco added with a wink, giving her a brotherly peck on the cheek. "Anyone else here?" he whispered in her ear.

"Just Antonia," she whispered back.

He lifted a speculative eyebrow. "Antonia, huh? Pretty?"

"Gorgeous. Short dark hair, huge brown eyes, a smile that could melt a snowman's heart and..."

"And?" Alessandro prompted, coming up behind them.

"And little bitty dimples on all four cheeks." They stared at her in shock, and barely able to suppress a smile, she led the way to the living room. "Can I get you anything to drink?"

"Come on, Grace," Stef pleaded. "Give. What's going on?"

She shook her head. "I can't tell. Besides, it's Luc's story."

"Pietro's story, to be exact," Luc corrected from the doorway.

The expressions on the four younger Salvatore brothers were all she could have hoped for. Ranging from bemusement to shock, they stared in absolute silence at the baby in Luc's arms. Alessandro was the first to recover.

"This is Antonia of the four dimples, I assume."

"Is she . . . *yours?*" Rocco asked in disbelief.

"Pietro's," Luc repeated.

Marc snapped his fingers. "Pietro and—what was her name . . . ? The little foreign-exchange student he was so crazy about. Carina! Is it hers?" He shook his head, not bothering to wait for confirmation. "I'll bet her parents had a thing or two to say when they heard about this little incident."

"You've met Carina?" Grace questioned in surprise.

"Once," he confirmed. "Briefly. Pietro was very protective. He didn't encourage me to stick around for long."

Stef nudged his twin in the ribs. "Afraid big brother would steal his love away?"

Marc grinned. "I would have, given half the chance. She's quite something."

"Why don't we get dinner started and I'll bring you up-to-date," Luc ordered.

Within minutes all five Salvatores were gathered in the kitchen, working as a well-orchestrated team to prepare dinner. Grace watched in amusement. They'd obviously done this before. Each took a different duty, occasionally asking Grace to pass a pot or a measuring cup or utensil. Toni, delighted to be the center of so much masculine attention, was passed from one set of arms to the next.

"Dinner will be in twenty minutes," Luc announced. "Marc, set the table." He turned to Grace. "And you, my fine beauty, may go change out of your office clothes and into something more festive. Tonight, I feel in the mood to celebrate.''

Four pairs of eyes, wide with astonishment, turned in Grace's direction. She could feel an intense blush blossom across her cheeks. Apparently, her masquerade was still a success with four of the five Salvatores present. She didn't know whether to be pleased or insulted.

Noticing his brothers' reactions, Luc explained, "Will-William, her fiancé, has her in disguise. For some reason, he wants her to look like a bag lady. I haven't quite figured out why. I will, though. I will.''

"A disguise?'' Stef asked, intrigued. "Like in the movies?''

Rocco approached. "You mean all I have to do is...''

Before she could protest, he whipped off her glasses. From behind, Alessandro slipped the pins from her hair, fluffing the wayward curls around her face and shoulders. "This isn't fair,'' she protested. "Stop it!'' Marc advanced next, and she knew from his mischievous grin that he intended to investigate what lay beneath her bulky wool suit.

Apparently, so did Luc. Sweeping her clear of his brothers' clutches, he gave her a gentle push toward the door. "Put on the green dress,'' he said.

And by the remorseless gleam in his golden eyes, she knew it wasn't a request.

CHAPTER SIX

The Great Lie
Still Day 338 and Grace's deception is fast unravel-
ing...

GRACE SPENT FIFTEEN of the next twenty minutes debating whether or not to wear the green dress. Upper-
most in her mind was Dom and his reaction should he
find out about her stay at Luc's. Did Luc's brothers
know she'd spent the previous night in this apartment—
or that she'd also be spending tonight here? If so, Dom
would learn the truth eventually from them. She couldn't
very well ask them not to mention it. What excuse could
she give?

She sank onto the edge of the bed. This was getting too
complicated. Perhaps she should give up her disguise. Or
what was left of her disguise. If Dom found out, she'd be
frank. She'd explain the situation to him and pray he'd
understand. After all, she'd only been trying to help his
family.

Despite that one rather tumultuous kiss, her relationship with Luc hadn't gotten too far out of hand—until
Toni's advent into their lives, they'd had no real personal involvement at all. Nor could she be blamed because Carina and Pietro had chosen to dump Toni in
Luc's lap and take off for parts unknown. What was she
supposed to have done? Refuse her aid? Leave Luc and

Toni to fend for themselves? It wasn't in her nature to be so cold and uncaring. Surely Dom wouldn't hold that against her.

Would he?

Giving up on such a fruitless debate, Grace reluctantly pulled the green dress from the closet. She'd bought it a month ago to wear home for Christmas. The trip was a gift to herself for having completed her year's sojourn at Salvatore's, and she'd wanted to treat herself to something special . . . something spectacular. And the silk dress was certainly that. Even shopping for it had been fun.

Without giving herself time to reconsider, she stripped off her suit and slipped on the dress. It was sheer perfection. Long-sleeved, with a fitted bodice and V neckline, the belled skirt floated to her knees. A string of pearls and earrings her parents had given her for her twenty-first birthday lent a final glamorous touch.

Crossing to the adjoining bathroom, she opened her cosmetic bag and applied a touch of makeup. It was always a pleasure slipping back into clothes that fit and wearing colors that flattered rather than detracted from her appearance. Stepping back from the mirror, she eyed the results with approval. Suddenly, she felt like herself again.

Next, she brushed out her hair. She assumed Alessandro still had her pins, so she'd have to leave it down. She tilted her head to one side. Swept back from a deep widow's peak, her hair framed her face and fell in soft curls to her shoulders. A good portion of the rinse had washed out, leaving interesting streaks of gold mixed in with the brown, as though her hair had been partially bleached by the sun. It actually looked quite attractive.

Slipping on a pair of heels, she left the bedroom and followed the sound of masculine voices to the dining room. Dinner had just been put on the table, the assorted bowls and platters steaming, a variety of delicious odors wafting in her direction.

Luc noticed her first. To her dismay, he didn't seem the least surprised by her altered appearance. With an annoying calm, he settled Toni more comfortably on his lap. But then a slow smile of satisfaction slid across his face and his eyes took on a gleam of hot intensity that shook her to the core. Had he known she'd look like this? she wondered uneasily. But how? Was it possible...? Had he seen through her disguise from the beginning? It was a frightening thought.

Rocco noticed her next, stumbling to a halt in midsentence. His mouth opened and closed, but he couldn't seem to get any words out. At that, all conversation stopped. If the varied reactions to Toni had been amusing, the reactions to Grace's transformation were even more so. Luc's brothers scrambled to their feet, tripping over themselves as they fought their way to her side. An instant later four large, gorgeous men had her completely surrounded.

It felt wonderful.

"Grace!"

"What the hell have you done to yourself?"

"Never mind that! What the hell were you doing running around looking like you did when you could have looked like... Damn!"

With a teasing grin, Marc threw himself at her feet. "Marry me, Grace!"

Alessandro turned to confront Luc. "You kept her all covered up on purpose. That's not fair."

Luc shrugged. "I told you. It wasn't my idea. Blame Will-William."

Marc gained his feet, a frown darkening his handsome face. "Your fiancé makes you dress like that? Like...like..."

"Like a bag lady," Luc supplied helpfully.

"He makes you dress like a bag lady?" Marc's frown grew darker. "What the hell for?"

"Yeah," Stef echoed, an identical frown lining his brow. "What the hell for?"

For the first time, Grace managed to get a word in edgewise. "To protect me from my boss," she deadpanned, trying to relieve the mounting tension. It hadn't occurred to her that they'd see her disguise in such an ominous light.

"To protect you?" Rocco questioned in astonishment.

"From Luc?"

"It worked, didn't it?" she said with an impish grin.

Her jest broke the mood, the four brothers bursting into laughter. Crossing to the table, she caught a brief glimpse of Luc's narrowed, thoughtful gaze. That one look was sufficient. She didn't dare glance his way again. It was as though a light bulb had just gone on in his head. She suspected that she'd given a little too much away with that last crack, and Luc had caught her slip.

Anxious to change the subject, she scooped Toni out of Luc's arms. "So, what do you think of your niece?" she asked the room at large.

Her question brought a slew of responses, each proud uncle attempting to outflatter the others. It was clear they adored the newest member of the family. Within minutes, she'd been snatched away from Grace, and even as they enjoyed their meal, Toni continued to be ensconced on one or the other of her uncles' laps. On the receiving end of so much adoration, she kicked her little legs and waved her hands, blinking adoringly into each handsome face.

"Flirt," Rocco announced in proud disgust. "It's a good thing you have so many uncles. You'll need them to beat off the boyfriends."

"So, when does Pietro return?" Alessandro asked.

"Soon, I hope," Luc responded. "Until he does, Grace has agreed to help me with Toni."

"You're staying here?" Marc questioned with an impudent grin.

Throwing a troubled glance Luc's way, she nodded. So much for keeping this episode from Dom. She could only hope he'd be reasonable. If she could continue to hold Luc at a distance, she didn't think there would be a problem. The only question being, could she do it? She hadn't realized how much she'd come to depend on her disguise for protection. With that blown, she'd just have to cling even tighter to the imaginary William.

"Yes," she said. "I'm using Luc's guest room until Pietro or Carina returns. Which reminds me . . ." She slipped from her chair and addressed Luc. "I need to call my fiancé and give him an update. Do you mind if I use the phone in your study?"

"Feel free." She couldn't read his expression, but somehow she suspected it held amusement. "Oh, and Grace . . ."

She glanced back over her shoulder. "Yes?"

This time she couldn't mistake his amusement. "Be sure and give him my regards."

The buzz of questions began the moment she stepped from the room. She didn't doubt for a minute they were about her and William. And from their tone, she also didn't doubt they were critical. Not that it mattered. A few more weeks and she could dispense with her engagement ring and be finished forever with lies and pretend engagements and futile disguises.

Sitting in Luc's study, she punched in her home phone number and spoke sheer drivel to her answering machine for the next ten minutes. Luc appeared in the doorway just as she'd cradled the receiver.

"How's Will-William?" he asked.

"Anxious for Carina and Pietro to return so our lives can get back to normal," she lied with composure.

He continued to stand in the doorway, blocking her only avenue of escape. "He's not concerned about your staying here?"

She lifted her chin. "Should he be?"

"I would, if I were your fiancé." He left the doorway and approached, standing directly in front of her chair. "In fact, I wouldn't allow you to spend five minutes in another man's apartment without me, let alone the entire night."

Anger sparked in her eyes. "But then, you're not my fiancé. And for the record, no man *allows* me to do anything. I do what I choose."

He smiled with a complacency that made her very, very nervous. "And you've chosen to stay with me."

"With Toni," she amended.

He let her correction slide without comment. Folding his arms across his chest, he tilted his head to one side. "Have I told you how beautiful you look tonight?"

"Thank you." She practically leapt from the chair, anxious to end this conversation and put some extra bodies between them. Nice, tall, protective bodies in the form of four Salvatore brothers. "Shall we join the others?" she suggested. He didn't move and to her distress, now that she was standing, they almost touched. Perhaps leaving the safety of the chair had been a mistake.

He lowered his head, asking softly, "Nervous, *cara?*"

She froze. "Not at all," she managed to say, wondering if she could edge around him and escape out the door. "But as you've just pointed out, I am engaged, and this conversation isn't appropriate."

He lifted an eyebrow. "No? What's inappropriate about it? The fact that I called you beautiful? Or the fact that we're here...alone...together?" A smile edged across his mouth. "We'll be alone tonight, and yet you just said that wasn't a problem."

"It's not!"

"Then perhaps it's that we're standing so close."

"Luc—"

"But that can't be it. We stand this close to each other at work all the time." His gaze dropped to the rapid rise and fall of her breasts. "Though I don't remember it having quite this effect on you." He captured her chin in his hand, his golden eyes once again on her face, watchful and dangerous. "Did it?"

"No!" she denied instantly. "It didn't. It still doesn't."

He tilted his head to one side. "You're lying," he told her bluntly. "You know how I can tell? Your eyes. Those clear, bright green eyes cloud over like a stormy sky when you aren't being honest. Is that why you wore those glasses? How many other lies have you told me while hiding behind a pair of tinted lenses, I wonder?"

"Luc, please..." she whispered.

"I want to please you." His voice was husky, deepening with an emotion she didn't dare try to identify. "You don't know how much I want to please you."

She bit her lip. "Our lives are complicated enough. Don't make it any worse."

"Worse? I'll make it better. Much, much better. Give it a chance, Grace. Give me a chance."

She was so very, very tempted. She shut her eyes and instantly a picture leapt to life. A picture of her mother sewing bits of lace and ribbon to the clever little stuffed animals she so lovingly created. "Baby dreams," she'd called them. And from that the idea for Baby Dream Toys had been born, a business they'd plotted and planned to someday open together. She shook her head. She couldn't do it. She couldn't sacrifice something so precious for a fleeting moment of pleasure. "No," she whispered, opening her eyes. "I can't. Let go of me, Luc. Please."

For a long minute he stood without speaking, his thoughtful gaze narrowed on her, as if trying to analyze something that defied analysis. His attention dropped briefly to her engagement ring and a small smile touched his mouth before he released her. "By all means. Join my brothers. They're about to leave, anyway." He moved toward the phone. "I want to make a quick call. I'll join you in a minute."

"All right." She hesitated, something in his face setting off warning bells. But she couldn't figure out why.

He picked up the receiver and raised an eyebrow in question. "Anything else?" he asked.

She shook her head, and without another word went in search of Luc's brothers. She found them grouped in the living room, slipping on coats and giving Toni good-bye hugs and kisses. Grace smiled. That little girl was going to grow up being very spoiled... and very much loved.

"Time to move out," Alessandro announced, throwing open the front door and handing Grace the baby.

"Look!" Marc exclaimed. "She smiled at me."

"So what?" his twin scoffed. "She's been doing that to me all evening."

"Only because she got the two of us mixed up."

Luc suddenly appeared, bringing up the rear. "Quiet down," he ordered. "And don't forget. No one is to know Toni's here. One run-in with the police was enough. We can't risk another."

"You got it."

"Mum's the word."

"Not a problem," Alessandro assured. "Oh, hello, Mrs. Bumgartle. Were we being too noisy again?"

A long, sharp nose poked around the doorway opposite. "This time I'm calling the manager. He'll take care of you hooligans. See if he doesn't!"

"I'm sorry, Mrs. Bumgartle," Luc said, crossing the hall to speak to her. "My brothers were just leaving. You won't hear another sound out of them." He threw a stern glance over his shoulder. "Right, boys?"

She peered at Luc, then at his brothers, her eyes narrow with dislike. "Hooligans, the lot of you!" And with that she slammed the door.

"Whoo-hoo," Marc said with a chuckle. "I do love seeing Mrs. Bumgartle. It reminds me there's one woman on this planet you can't charm."

"Two women," Stef corrected. "You're forgetting about Cynthia. Remember? The tall, gorgeous brunette? Totally immune. She could freeze Luc dead in his tracks with one look."

Rocco slapped Luc on the back. "Don't worry, big brother. Two out of millions. We won't hold it against you."

Luc grinned. "Get out of here, before I knock some heads together. I'll let you know when I hear from Pietro."

The four trooped toward the elevator and Grace lifted the baby to her shoulder. "I think that's enough excitement for one day. Time for bed, young lady," she announced and slipped back into Luc's apartment.

Across the hall, the door opened again. "Good night, Mrs. Bumgartle," Luc called cheerfully. The door crashed shut and with a shrug he followed Grace into the apartment.

"Did you speak to her about yesterday?" she asked, moving over to the picture windows in the living room. "I don't want her to put the wrong connotation on anything she might have overheard."

He shook his head. "I never got the chance. It doesn't matter. She makes empty threats all the time."

Grace frowned. "Still..."

"Forget about Mrs. Bumgartle." He came to stand next to her, dropping an arm around her shoulders, wrapping her and the baby in a protective embrace.

She gazed at the window, fascinated by the image reflected there. They might have been a real family. Luc towered above her, elegant and broad shouldered in black trousers and a pullover sweater. Her soft green skirt seemed to cling to his legs with a life of its own. And Toni gurgled, her arms pumping the air as though trying to catch hold of him.

"Tell me, Grace." His hand slipped along the nape of her neck and he caught a fistful of streaked curls in his hand. "Is it my imagination, or is your hair lighter?"

She stiffened against him, hastily ducking to press a kiss to the top of Toni's head. "Does it seem lighter?" she asked in a muffled voice, tufts of soft black hair tickling her lips. "I hadn't noticed."

"Don't play games with me, Grace." His voice acquired a rough, impatient edge. "You've been coloring it. Why?"

She shrugged. "It's a woman's prerogative, isn't it?"

"To go from gold to mud brown?" he asked derisively. "Of course. It makes perfect sense."

She attempted to step free of his arms, but he still held her hair clenched in his fist and for a moment she didn't think he'd let go. "I'd like to put Toni down," she said quietly.

He opened his hand, releasing her. "I'll help."

She knew better than to argue when he used that tone. She inclined her head in agreement and led the way to the guest room, which was rapidly being converted into a dream nursery. A changing table now stood near the gleaming white crib—both special deliveries from a nearby furniture store. Next to the changing table hung a Toys-a-Trillion pet net, a triangular hammock that attached to the wall and held every conceivable stuffed animal.

Laying Toni on the changing table, Grace wound up a music box to keep the baby entertained while she took care of the lengthy process of putting on dry diapers and slipping a wiggly baby into pajamas.

"Why don't you sleep in my bed tonight."

Grace started, jabbing herself with the diaper pin. "Ouch!" She glared at Luc, holding up a wounded finger. "Look what you made me do."

A lazy grin drifted across his mouth. "You want me to kiss it better?"

"Not a chance." She snatched a damp baby wipe from its plastic box and wrapped it around her finger. "And just to clarify... That 'not a chance' is in response to both of your requests. You know I won't sleep with you. I'm engaged."

"So you keep reminding me. But, I don't recall asking you to sleep with me, though if you're offering..."

"I'm not," she snapped, carrying Toni from the changing table to the crib. "Then what were you asking?"

"Offering, not asking. I'm offering my bed. It's my turn to get up with Toni for the middle-of-the-night feeding and diaper change. So either we push the crib into my room or I sleep in here."

"Don't worry about it," she said, dismissing his concerns. "I'll take care of Toni. You stay right where you are."

He shook his head, a crooked smile drifting across his mouth. "Sorry. I can't do that." He switched off the lamp on the nightstand. A silly clown face night-light glowed near the crib, holding the darkness at bay. He moved toward her, his shadow leaping across the wall, joining with hers. "It wouldn't be fair."

"I don't mind," she insisted.

"I do." He caught her hand and tugged her out of the room. "Come on. We'll go back to the living room and argue about it there."

"Luc..."

"You don't want to argue about who takes care of Toni tonight?"

"Not really."

Refusing to let go of her hand, he crossed to the couch, pulling her down next to him. "Then we'll argue about the real reason for the disguise you've been hiding behind for almost a year."

"Why don't we talk about the weather," she suggested dryly, moving to the far side of the couch. "That's always a nice, safe topic."

"The weather? Fine." He closed the distance between them, crowding her against the cushions. "I sense a sudden heat wave. How about you?"

She pressed her hands to his chest, aware that she'd just as soon wrap her arms around him as push him away. "Luc, cut it out. This isn't a scene out of some 1940s romantic comedy, you know."

"You're right." He reached past her and turned off the lamp on the table behind them. Instantly, the room plunged into darkness. "Now it's a scene out of a 1940s romantic comedy," he murmured, his mouth nuzzling her ear. Moonlight filtered in through the picture windows and bathed them in a silvery glow. "The seduction scene to be exact."

Her breath stopped in her throat. He was so close, practically lying on top of her. "And I thought talking about the weather would be safe. I'm beginning to think there aren't any safe topics with you," Grace said.

"Then let's not talk."

"Don't, Luc. I don't want this."

"I think you do. Shall I tell you what else I think?" He didn't wait for her answer. His hand tangled in her hair, the streaked curls spilling from between his fingers. "I think you dyed your hair and wore suits three sizes too large for a reason."

"What reason?" she asked, feeling alarmed.

"For the same reason behind this." He lifted her left hand and touched her engagement ring. "For protection."

She stared at him in shock. Did he know? Had she given herself away? She fought his hold. "You're crazy."

"Am I?" His arms moved around her, pulling her tight. "You could be right about that. Let's be crazy together."

He didn't say any more. He simply lowered his head and kissed her. In that instant, she realized that her reaction to their first kiss hadn't been a fluke. It was as if someone had thrown on a main power switch. Her senses came on-line, leaping to life with a jarring force that swept away all resistance, all thought, leaving only a desperate need behind, raw and undeniable.

His kiss stole her breath, stole her will, and she almost groaned aloud. He tasted wonderful, as heady as fine champagne. One sip and her palate was forever jaded, never again to be satisfied with anything but the best. And he was the best.

He broke off the kiss and shifted closer, his weight pressing her deep into the cushions, his body hard and taut against hers. She gazed up at him, wanting him to kiss her again but unable to ask, afraid of the words— afraid of the desire such words would express. His thick hair tumbled across his brow and he stared at her, his eyes no longer golden but two glittering shards of jet.

"You're safe with me," he murmured, and she knew he'd sensed her fears as well as her desire. "I won't hurt you, Grace, I swear it."

He kissed her again and she tilted her head, exposing the long line of her neck. His mouth drifted downward, following the deep V of her dress. Tenderly, he cupped her breast, caressing, stoking the fires that raged within her, driving her toward a sweet ecstasy she'd never before experienced.

"Come to my bed, Grace," he urged. "Let me show you how good it can be between us."

She wanted to. Oh, how she wanted to. But it would be wrong, for so many reasons. His mouth found hers again, tantalizing her with teasing little kisses, until all she could think or feel was a desperate craving for more. Lord, he was good at this. Unfortunately, that indicated he'd had plenty of practice. Which meant...

"Luc..." she forced herself to say. "This isn't smart. We can't do this."

He laughed with genuine humor, the sound warm and beguiling. "Of course we can. I've wanted to do this for ages. Haven't you?"

She shied away from his question, asking one of her own instead. "If you wanted to do this for so long, then why haven't you?"

He hesitated, then shrugged. "There were...roadblocks."

As far as she knew, most of the roadblocks remained. He might suspect her engagement to William was an invention. But he had no real proof. And though he wasn't aware that her agreement with Dom prevented a personal relationship with him, their business association should be more than enough to give him pause before starting a...a *fling*.

"And now there aren't any roadblocks?" she questioned.

He eyed her closely. "You tell me."

She didn't dare mention William or Dom. "What about my job?" she asked instead, seizing on the one obstacle they could openly discuss.

"What about it? It's not going anywhere."

"What about after we...? What happens to my job, then?"

He pulled back and frowned. "What the hell does that mean?"

She shook her head. "You think I haven't heard about my predecessors? There must be a regular army of women who've left your employment because they fell in love with you."

"For your information, I have never had an affair with anyone who worked for me."

"Until now?"

The question seemed to hang between them. For a minute she didn't think he'd respond. Then he nodded. "Until now," he conceded roughly. He cupped her face and kissed her with a desperate urgency, as though he wanted to drive all thought, all resistance, from her mind. She almost allowed herself to give in to desire, to allow him to sweep aside all concerns but a selfish need to be loved.

In that instant, she saw her choices more clearly than she ever had before. She could break all the rules she held dear and have a few brief, stolen moments with Luc—and they'd be wonderful memories, memories she'd retain for the rest of her life. But then his interest would move on to the next woman and he'd break her heart. Or she could stop the relationship now, before it went any further.

In a few weeks, Dom would return and she'd leave Luc's employment. Maybe she'd experience a few regrets—maybe more than a few. But she'd have Baby Dream Toys. More important, there was still a slim chance she could emerge from this with her heart intact. Which left her only one option.

Now all she had to do was find a way to distance Luc.

Not giving him time to realize what she intended, she ripped free of his embrace and stood. "Why are you doing this?" she demanded, driven by sheer self-preservation to take the offensive. "I'm your employee, trying to help you out of an awkward situation. And you're—you're attacking me."

He lifted an eyebrow, his expression amused. "What a vivid imagination you have. Do you really consider what I did attacking you?"

"Yes! No!" She'd never succeed at putting him off if she couldn't do better than that. There was only one out available, and she'd darned well better take it. She lifted her chin and folded her arms across her chest. Using her most businesslike voice, she said, "If you want to continue having my help, you'll keep our relationship professional. I don't want you to make suggestive remarks or—or touch me. If you do, I'll leave. Is that clear?"

She held her breath, praying that this time he'd believe her, believe what was fast becoming more and more of a lie. To her distress she realized that, despite the choice she'd made, she didn't want just a professional relationship with Luc. And far from finding his remarks suggestive, she found them romantic and all too appealing. She shied away from thinking about his touch, and the fact that she'd begun to crave each casual caress with a passion that frightened her. She had to remember Baby Dream Toys and her mother. She *had* to.

He sat up, his expression unreadable. "It's clear." He studied her for several minutes, as though trying to understand what had gone wrong, and then his voice softened. "There's no need to be afraid, you know. We can take this slow. If I'm rushing you, you set the pace."

With a quick shake of her head, she said, "I'm not interested in setting any pace."

"Except a full retreat?" Irony colored his words.

"Shall I go pack?"

He held up his hands. "You win. If you don't want to see where this might lead, I won't push it."

"Thank you." There wasn't anything left to be said. Without another word, she headed from the room.

"Grace?"

She hesitated, but didn't turn around, waiting for him to say what he had to so she could finally escape. "What is it, Luc?"

"I don't want to lose you. So I won't touch you again, if that's your preference."

"Thank you," she said again.

"Don't thank me. It's not what I'd do if the choice were mine. If you were honest with yourself, you'd admit it isn't really what you want, either." His voice held a grating quality she'd never heard before. "And one more thing."

"Yes?" she whispered.

"Take my bed."

She turned around at that. "No! That's—that's not necessary."

Slowly he rose from the couch and she realized to her dismay that a very large, frustrated man stood before her. "Take my bed," he repeated.

"Fine." She swallowed nervously, backing from the room. "I'll take your bed."

He stalked after her. "And for your information, *bellissima mia,* just so there isn't any doubt in your mind... All through that passionate little speech your eyes were as cloudy as I've ever seen them. Run away for now, but don't leave thinking I believed a word you said. You do want me. And soon, very soon, you'll admit it to yourself... and to me."

She didn't dare say another word. Instead, she turned on her heels and ran.

CHAPTER SEVEN

The Great Lie
Day 339 and trouble is at the door...

LOCKING HERSELF IN LUC's room did nothing to make Grace feel safe. Standing by the bed, she wondered how in the world she could be expected to sleep here. She didn't even have her pajamas. Darn him! She didn't even have a toothbrush. Nor did she have any intention of going after the forgotten items.

As though in answer to her silent raging, a brief knock sounded at the door. It could only be Luc. As she stood motionless, debating whether or not to open it, the knob turned. She heard his muffled laugh as he realized she'd locked him out.

"If you want your nightgown, it's here," he informed her through the wooden panel. "Feel free to use my toothbrush. Good night, Grace. Pleasant dreams."

She waited several minutes before opening the door. Sure enough, her gown and robe lay neatly folded on the rug. Luc was nowhere in sight. She crossed to his dresser and rummaged through drawers until she found a pair of pajamas. Returning to the hallway, she swapped nightclothes and slammed the door shut, locking it once again. As far as a toothbrush was concerned ... use his? Not likely. It was bad enough that she had to use his bed.

Stripping off her dress, she tossed it across a chair and glared at the pool of soft green silk. In her mind's eye she saw Luc's hand against the pale dress as he cupped her breast, his dark hair contrasting with her white skin as he bent to... She struggled to breathe normally. Maybe she wouldn't wear the dress for Christmas, after all. Maybe she wouldn't wear it ever again.

A few minutes later she was ready for bed, her teeth brushed with her finger and a bit of toothpaste. She wondered if she'd get any sleep. Doubtful, considering how everything in the room served to remind her of Luc—and the passion they'd shared... almost shared. It had to be Luc's not-so-subtle way of tormenting her.

The worst part came when she slipped between his sheets and rested her head on his pillow. His spicy scent clung to the pillowcase, filling her lungs with every breath and arousing emotions she'd sooner forget. She clenched her fists. He'd done this on purpose. He wanted to drive her insane. Well, it wouldn't work.

Three hours later, and on the verge of true madness, she started to drift off to sleep. An urgent banging put paid to that. Totally disoriented, it took her several seconds to realize the pounding came not from outside her bedroom but from outside the apartment. Grabbing her robe, she thrust her arms into it as she dashed for the door. For endless moments she fumbled with the lock and by the time she'd reached the hallway, Luc raced just ahead of her. Wearing the pajama bottoms she'd left out for him, he opened the front door, running a hand through his hair.

"What—" he began.

To Grace's horror, she saw a pair of policemen standing there, Mrs. Bumgartle right behind them, a self-righteous expression on her face.

"Arrest him," Mrs Bumgartle demanded, pointing an accusing finger at Luc. "Arrest them both! Those... those... those babynappers!"

For a long moment, no one moved. Then Luc asked, "What's the problem, Officer?"

"Mr. Salvatore? I'm Officer Hatcher. We met two days ago at your office."

"I remember," Luc replied evenly. "Is there a problem?"

"Babynapper!" Mrs. Bumgartle proclaimed from behind the policeman's broad shoulders. "He said the baby was his niece—that she was his brother's child. But all his brothers visited tonight and she wasn't theirs. And he—" she pointed a finger at Luc with dramatic emphasis "—warned them that they couldn't afford to have the police called in again."

Officer Hatcher glanced from Luc to a clearly nervous Grace. "Perhaps I better come in and straighten this out. Carl," he addressed his partner, "escort Mrs. Bumgartle to her apartment and take a statement."

After a momentary hesitation, Luc stepped back to allow the policeman access. Though he didn't say anything, Grace saw the muscle leaping in his jaw and the dark, furious glitter of his eyes. Why, oh why, she wondered with a sinking heart, did it have to be Hatcher who responded to the call?

"There's nothing to straighten out," Luc insisted, leading the way to the living room. "I explained before that we were baby-sitting my niece and that's precisely what we're doing."

Hatcher pulled a notepad out of his pocket and flipped through the pages. "According to my notes, you said you were baby-sitting for a few hours. It's now been almost two days. Would you care to explain the discrepancy?"

Luc glanced briefly at Grace, then said, "I believe I mentioned that my sister-in-law's mother is ill. My brother and his wife were going to fly to Italy with the baby, but decided at the last minute to leave Toni with us." He caught Grace's hand in his and pulled her close. "Is that a problem?"

Officer Hatcher began adding to his notes. "You have something from the parents stating this?"

"No," Luc admitted. "I didn't realize that would be necessary."

The policeman's gaze sharpened. "A medical release form? A birth certificate? Anything?"

Luc shook his head. "They should be back soon."

Hatcher glanced at his notes again and froze. "How old is your niece, Mr. Salvatore? What's her birth-date?"

Grace started, staring up at Luc in a panic. His arm tightened around her, crushing her to his side. "She's three months," Luc said stiffly. "I'm ... I'm not sure of the exact date of her birth."

"And when did her sex change from male to female?" Hatcher asked with unmistakable sarcasm. He had them and he knew it.

Luc swore beneath his breath.

"You didn't know she was a girl, did you?" The patrolman's mouth twisted in a parody of a smile. "Is she even your niece?"

"I didn't know she was a girl until we changed her diaper," Luc was forced to concede. "Carina called her Toni, and since Salvatores have a history of producing boys, I assumed..." He shrugged, then stated forcefully, "But she *is* my niece."

Officer Hatcher checked his notes again. "The baby's name is Antonia Donati . . . Salvatore? Or was that a lie, too?"

Luc closed his eyes, releasing a long, drawn-out sigh. "Carina and my brother aren't married. Yet. I expect that to change very soon."

"Let me get this straight." The officer's words fell, cold and hard as chipped ice. "You said the parents left the baby in your care and would be back in a few hours. That was a lie. You said the child was your nephew. That was a lie. And you said the baby's parents were married. Another lie. You don't have any legal authority to care for this baby whatsoever, do you?"

Luc's fists clenched at his sides. "Look. Carina, the baby's mother, left Toni with my brother because of a family emergency. That much is true. And she needed someone to care for Toni during her absence. That is also the truth. Since my brother Pietro is the baby's father, he was the natural choice. The only problem was, Pietro didn't know about Toni until Carina arrived at my office."

Understanding dawned. "Which explains the argument in the lobby."

"Yes. My brother went after Carina to try and stop her. Thanks to your intervention, he wasn't in time."

Grace winced. "Luc, it won't help to antagonize him," she murmured.

"I don't care," he snapped. "If the police hadn't been so quick to let Carina go, we wouldn't be in our current predicament. Not that it matters. When Pietro does catch up with her, they'll marry and return for Toni. Until then, my fiancée and I are taking care of the baby. She's perfectly safe and in good hands."

"That's not for me to decide."

Luc stiffened. "What the hell does that mean?"

"Easy," Grace murmured, laying a restraining hand on Luc's arm.

"No!" He shook free of her hold. "I want to know what he means."

Hatcher eyed them sternly. "I mean that what happens to the baby is up to social services, not me. Legally, she's been abandoned."

"No, she hasn't!" Luc bit out. "The mother left her child with the father."

"Mr. Salvatore, I don't intend to argue with you about this. I'm taking the baby into custody. If you resist, I'll arrest you."

Before Luc could respond, Grace asked, "What will happen to Toni?"

Hatcher explained while writing. "The law requires we have her transported by ambulance to the local hospital. She'll be examined there and kept overnight at the child-protection center. In the morning they'll put her in a temporary foster home while an emergency-response worker investigates the case." He spoke by rote, his demeanor cool and dispassionate, repeating an explanation he'd obviously given before.

"How do we get her back?" Grace questioned.

He hesitated, glancing up. For the first time, his guard relaxed slightly. "To be honest, I'm not sure you can. The best chance you have is to get in touch with the legal guardian—presumably the mother—and obtain a signed custody statement and a medical-permission slip. A copy of the birth certificate wouldn't hurt, either."

Grace gazed at Luc. "Can we do that?" she whispered.

He gave a brief nod. "Pietro can fax it to us."

"Even then, it's questionable whether the authorities will release her to you. Though—" Hatcher hesitated, eyeing Grace "—a *permanent* female presence in the home could possibly tip the scales in your favor." He snapped his notepad closed and pocketed it. "Take me to the baby."

There was nothing they could do after that. Luc went into the spare bedroom and packed a diaper bag with several days' worth of clothes, diapers and baby paraphernalia. Fighting back tears, Grace carefully bundled up Toni for the trip into the frigid night air. The entire time, Officer Hatcher stood in the doorway, watching their every move.

"Wait." She stopped Luc before he could close the diaper bag. Handing him the baby, she grabbed a floppy-eared rabbit from the pet net and thrust it in among the clothes he'd packed. "What about a bottle and a spare can of formula?" she asked the policeman.

"Can't hurt."

"It'll only take a minute." She glanced at Luc. He held Toni, his face expressionless, but she could sense his impotent fury. "Officer Hatcher, would you mind helping me?" She sent Hatcher a pleading look, hoping against hope that he'd give Luc the few moments of privacy he needed to say goodbye to Toni.

After a brief hesitation, the policeman nodded. "Two minutes. No more."

Chattering nonsense while she prepared a bottle, Grace prayed that Luc wouldn't do anything foolish. To her relief, he appeared in the doorway just as she'd finished mixing the formula. Without a word, he handed the officer the baby and the diaper bag.

"Here's my business card," Luc said. "My home phone number's on the back. I'll expect the emergency-response worker's call first thing in the morning." It wasn't a request.

Hatcher inclined his head. "I suggest you get those papers together and fast. You haven't a prayer otherwise."

And with that he left, Toni gently cradled in his arms.

The minute the door closed behind him, Luc slammed his fist against the wall, knocking a hole in the plaster. Grace came up behind, not sure approaching him at this time was the wisest course of action. "It's all right," she murmured. "We'll get her back."

He turned on her, his eyes wild with fury, dark color streaking across his angled cheekbones. "I won't let it happen again, Grace. I won't let them split up my family again."

Again. She stared at him in alarm. "What do you mean, again?" He didn't answer. Instead, he headed for the guest room, forcing her to run to keep up with him. "Luc?"

He crossed to the empty crib, spinning the colorful mobile with a surprisingly gentle hand. Removing Toni's crumpled pink blanket, he folded it and tossed it across the headboard. He'd cut himself hitting the wall; a streak of blood oozed from his bruised and scraped knuckles. If it bothered him, he gave no indication.

"I was fourteen when Pietro was born," he began. "I guess you'd call my brother an afterthought, though Mom and Dad were delighted by the addition. He'd make it an even half dozen, they'd say. The first time I saw him, I thought he was the ugliest creature ever created. I called him 'monkey face.'"

Grace curled up in the rocker near the crib and watched him with concern. She'd stumbled across something—she didn't quite know what—but at a guess it had a great deal to do with his feelings for Toni. "Pietro's looks have improved with age," she said lightly.

To her surprise a brief grin creased his face. "Yeah. They did." The grin faded. "Mom died when he was only a couple of months old."

"Oh, no," Grace cried softly.

He swatted at the mobile again, sending the cartoon characters careening in a drunken circle. "I'm not sure whether it was the stress of Pietro's birth—she was in her forties by the time she had him—or the pneumonia that killed her. Who knows? Maybe it was a combination of the two. Not that it matters now."

"Where was Dom?"

"Dad was in Italy on business. We had trouble contacting him." His voice deepened, the sound raspy with emotion. "Mom had all that information, but she went so fast she didn't have time to tell us how..."

She left the rocker and crossed to his side. "What happened?" she asked, slipping her arms around his waist and resting her cheek against his broad back. His skin felt warm and smooth beneath her face.

He didn't push her away. Instead, he drew a deep breath. "Same as tonight. The police arrived to take us into foster care until Dad could come for us. I fought them. I mean, physically fought them."

He sounded so cold and remote, so removed from his memories. But she knew it was a false impression. She could hear the harsh sound of his breathing, feel his tension beneath her hands. "Why did you fight?" she asked.

"Family unity was drummed into us from the cradle. My mother's last request was that I keep everyone together until Dad returned. But the police wanted to separate us. I couldn't let them do that."

"You did your best, Luc," she said urgently. "You were so young. Too young to care for an infant, to supervise four rambunctious boys."

His hands fisted on the bars of the crib. "I was in charge. It was my duty to keep us all together until Dad came home. I tried. Heaven knows, I tried. But I didn't succeed. They took my brothers. Alessandro, the twins, Rocco and Pietro. They needed three policemen to hold me down while they got them all out of the house." He closed his eyes, swallowing hard. "We were dispersed to various foster homes. Three weeks later Dad returned."

"He didn't blame you?" she asked in alarm.

"Never. But I knew I'd failed. I won't fail again. I swear, I'll do anything—*anything*—to regain custody of Toni until Carina and Pietro get back."

"What are you planning?" she asked uneasily.

He turned in her arms, gazing down at her, his eyes dark with a passionate intensity. "You and I," he informed her in a hard, determined voice, "are now officially married."

"You *can't* be serious," she exclaimed, taking a quick step back.

His hands dropped to her shoulders, holding her in place. "I'm dead serious. Hatcher said having a permanent female presence in the house might tip the scales in our favor, and that's just what I intend to have."

"But what about Will ... William?"

"What about him?" he demanded.

There was a recklessness about Luc that worried her, and her gaze slid nervously from his. Perhaps this wasn't the best time to mention her supposed fiancé. "I'll ... discuss it with him."

"Yeah. You do that. In the meantime, I want as much of your stuff over here as we can carry. When Miss

Emergency Response Worker arrives on my doorstep, I want her to find a happily married couple—his-and-hers hairbrushes on the dresser, our toothbrushes sharing a tube of toothpaste and my shoes playing footsie with yours on the closet floor.''

If only she had time to think, time to line up all the reasons why his plan wouldn't work. She pulled from his grasp and tightened the sash of her robe, thrusting her hair back from her face. ''In case it escaped your notice, I haven't agreed to your request.''

He turned on her. ''Are you refusing your help?''

Was she? She frowned, eyeing the empty crib with a sick feeling in the pit of her stomach. With each passing hour, Luc drew her further and further into his personal problems. When Dom returned, could she face him honestly and say that she'd kept their agreement? But then, how could she leave Luc in such dire straits? How could she desert him?

''Do we have to claim we're married?'' she asked. ''The police think we're engaged. What happens if they compare notes?''

''Then we'll show them our marriage certificate.''

She stared at Luc in shock. *''What?''*

''Tomorrow we apply for a license and have all the required testing done, just in case a temporary marriage is necessary.''

''No! I won't do it.''

He approached, towering over her, his face set in hard, determined lines. ''Oh, yes, you will. I don't care what it takes. I'll give you whatever you want, but you will do this. If not for me, for Toni.''

She faced him defiantly. ''You have such a way with words.''

He inhaled deeply, pain etching deep furrows across his brow. "I'm sorry. I know I'm doing this all wrong. But... Please, Grace. I need you. I need your help. I can't let them take Toni away."

She closed her eyes, knowing she should turn him down flat. A strident voice of logic told her there wasn't a single valid reason for helping him, and every reason in the world for refusing. If she was smart, she'd listen to that voice. If she was smart...

"All right," she whispered. "I'll do it."

And then he kissed her, a kiss of such passion and heat that it was more than enough to still even the voice of logic.

THE PHONE WOKE her at the crack of dawn that morning. Grace crawled out of bed, every weary muscle in her body making her painfully aware that she'd hardly slept a wink after the police had left. Once again, she pulled on her robe and trudged toward the study.

"Pietro!" she heard Luc exclaim. "Where are you? *What! Épazzo!* What the *hell* are you doing back in Italy?"

"What's going on?" she asked, fighting back a yawn. "What's Pietro doing in Italy?"

Luc covered the mouthpiece. "Trying my patience." He spoke into the phone again. "Listen up, it's gotten serious here. The police came last night and took Toni."

She winced, able to hear Pietro's furious protests clear across the room. "Tell him we need a custody statement," she urged.

"Shut up and listen," Luc snapped.

She couldn't hide her hurt. "I was just trying to help."

"No, not you, Grace. Pietro. Come again? Never mind what she's doing here at this hour. It's what you have to do that's important."

Grace closed her eyes and groaned. Just when she'd thought matters couldn't get any worse, fate...or in this case Luc Salvatore...proved her wrong.

"You know that if it's within my powers I'll get Toni back, but we need a signed custody statement from Carina and a medical-permission slip. Can you get her to give them to you?"

Grace crossed to Luc's side. "Don't forget the birth certificate," she reminded him.

"Right. And a copy of Toni's birth certificate. You fax me the documents as soon as possible, is that clear? Otherwise, they'll put your daughter in a foster home and you'll have a hell of a time getting custody again."

Grace tugged at Luc's arm. He glanced down at her, exhaustion lining his face. Clearly, he hadn't slept, either. "Tell him it'll be okay," she said. "Tell him to take care of Carina and we'll take care of Toni. Reassure him."

He nodded briefly. "Don't worry, Pietro. You know I'll take care of everything. Just get home as soon as you can." After exchanging a few more words, he hung up. "Get dressed," he ordered Grace briskly. "If we're going to get Toni home tonight, we've got a list of chores a mile long to accomplish beforehand."

First on his list turned out to be moving as many of her belongings as possible to his apartment. In no time, they'd practically stripped her place bare and filled up his car with personal possessions.

Jingling the car keys in his pocket, he stood by her front door. "Ready?" he asked, obviously impatient to get to the second item on his list—the marriage license.

"I'll be right out," she said, suddenly remembering her answering machine. Who knew when she'd return to her apartment. She'd better check messages before she left. She didn't doubt there'd be at least one from her father.

To her dismay, there were three. Each one urged her to call home, that he had a surprise for her. Well, the surprise would have to wait until her situation returned to normal. Next on the tape was her ridiculous conversation with the fictitious William. Shooting a nervous glance over her shoulder, she fast-forwarded through the nonsensical spiel. To her horror, right after her monologue came a message from Luc.

"Well, well..." he practically purred into the tape. "How very interesting."

She stared at the machine in confusion. What...? Then she remembered the call he'd made in the study—right on the heels of her own. Did his phone have one of those buttons that automatically redialed the last number called? She struggled to remember. She could check, but she was about ninety-percent positive there had been. Which meant that after she'd supposedly chatted with her "fiancé," Luc had pushed the redial button and discovered that far from calling William, she'd phoned her own apartment.

She shut her eyes. No wonder he'd questioned the existence of any remaining roadblocks. With her disguise stripped away and his discovery that William didn't exist, he must have figured the road was perfectly clear—clear for seduction.

"Grace! Move it, will you?"

She jumped. How could she face him? What could she possibly say? "Coming!" she called.

She'd just have to muddle through the best she could. He must have left the message deliberately, so she'd know he knew. And now that she did...and he did... She groaned, covering her face. Maybe she could pretend she hadn't listened to the messages. She could give him her most innocent look and pray her eyes didn't go all cloudy or any such nonsense. Yes. That's what she'd do. Hadn't she gotten rather good at these sorts of fibs?

"What the hell is taking so long?" Luc strode into the room.

Oops.

His gaze moved from her answering machine to her bright red face and for the first time that day he grinned. "Something you forgot to tell me?"

"Not a thing," she declared, leaping to her feet. "Shall we go?"

He stood in front of her, his arms folded across his chest. "Not until you admit there is no William."

She lifted her chin. "Of course, there's a William." Whipping past him before he could stop her, she headed for the door. "I just don't happen to be engaged to him."

With a bark of laughter, Luc followed.

The next few hours passed in a mad dash. After setting the wheels in motion for a quickie wedding should the need arise, Luc purchased a wedding band for Grace, overriding her heated objections with callous determination.

"I don't have time to argue with you about this," he informed her impatiently, shoving the ring over her knuckle. "You've pretended to be engaged for the past eleven months. Now you're pretending to be married. What's the difference?"

She glared at him. "Give me a minute and I'll tell you."

"We don't have a minute. The emergency-response worker assigned to our case is meeting us at the apartment at noon. That doesn't give us much time to get everything in place.''

Realizing her arguments were fruitless in the face of such overwhelming resolve, she gave up and returned with Luc to his apartment. At the stroke of twelve she positioned the last of her personal possessions, and as if in response, the doorbell rang. Joining Luc at the door, they welcomed the social worker together.

Ms. Cartwright proved to be a very pleasant, no-nonsense careerwoman in her late thirties, and it took Luc precisely three minutes to totally charm her.

The first minute they exchanged names and business cards. Luc introduced Grace as his wife and thanked Ms. Cartwright for taking the time out of her busy schedule to visit with them.

The second minute, he fired a thousand questions about Toni's well-being at the startled woman.

The third minute, he relaxed, apologized for his abruptness and offered her one of his most stunning smiles. Grace had long ago realized that his smile could melt steel. Melting Ms. Cartwright was a cinch compared to that. Drawing her into the living room, he focused both that smile and his intense golden eyes on the hapless woman.

''You see,'' Luc explained, and there was no mistaking the rough sincerity in his voice, ''Toni is family. You tell me what I have to do to get her back here until her parents return from Italy and I'll do it. Anything.''

Ms. Cartwright visibly softened. ''Please understand, Mr. Salvatore. We aren't trying to split your family apart. We just want what's best for the child.''

He inclined his head in satisfaction. ''Then we have the same goal. I think you'll find what's best is for Toni to be returned to her family. Let me show you around and then we'll discuss what needs to be done."

Ms. Cartwright inspected every inch of the apartment with a nerve-racking thoroughness. Eventually, she wandered into their temporary nursery. "Why, what a beautiful room you have here," she said, pausing in the doorway. "You did all this for your niece?"

"Not just for Toni," Luc claimed, shooting an openly smoldering look in Grace's direction. "I was hoping to give her cousins sometime soon."

Ms. Cartwright beamed, patting Grace's arm. "I can tell by that blush that you're a newlywed. Ben Hatcher referred to you as Mr. Salvatore's fiancée in his report. You must have married recently?"

"Very," Luc answered for Grace.

The social worker made a brief notation on her clipboard. "I'm glad to hear that. I rarely approve a home where the primary caretakers aren't married. And who would have the main responsibility for Toni during the day?"

"We both would," Luc said. "I've arranged to work out of the apartment until my brother and his wife return."

"Wife?" Ms. Cartwright frowned. "I understood that Ms. Donati was a single parent. In fact, I'm a little concerned that you first told the police that your brother and Ms. Donati were married, then later admitted that wasn't true."

A variety of emotions chased across Luc's face...frustration, anger and finally resignation. "To be honest, Ms. Cartwright, I would have said just about anything to keep Toni with her family," he confessed in a low voice. "I know it's a terrible admission, but my brother had entrusted Toni to my care and I didn't want to let him down."

"I understand your feelings, but I must insist on absolute honesty from now on." The social worker was serious. She tapped her pencil against the clipboard, and Grace knew without question there'd be no charming her into overlooking any future fibs. "Lying to the police, or to us for that matter, is a grave offense. If we uncover any further...discrepancies, you will not be permitted to care for your niece now or any time in the future. Are we clear on this?"

Grace thought she'd pass out at the woman's feet. She didn't dare look at Luc. Instead, she stood as still as possible, fighting to keep from toying nervously with her phony wedding band. How had she managed to get herself into this mess? Maybe she'd phone her father, after all. She needed a good, strong dose of his common sense and principles. One of his lectures wouldn't go amiss around about now, either.

Luc weathered the imminent crisis far better. He forked his fingers through his hair and then inclined his head. "We're clear," he said.

Ms. Cartwright didn't seem to notice anything wrong. She examined the pages attached to her clipboard and said, "I'm also concerned about the mother in this case."

"Carina is young and rather emotional," Luc offered, stepping into the breach once again. "She wasn't thinking straight when she left Toni with us. She'd just had a baby out of wedlock—something both her family and her religion frown on. And she'd just learned her mother was on death's door. The one smart thing she did was to come to my brother for help."

"But he left the baby, too."

"In my custody. I'm the eldest, and my brothers have always come to me when they needed help. Look, Ms. Cartwright. I'm positive they'll marry very soon and return to straighten all this out. If social services wants to investigate me to ensure I'm a fit temporary guardian for Toni, then fine. If they want to camp out on my doorstep in order to keep an eye on me, they're welcome. All I ask is that you let me take care of Toni until Carina and Pietro get back."

His impassioned speech clearly had an affect on Ms. Cartwright. "You make a very eloquent case for yourself, Mr. Salvatore," she said with a sigh.

"That was my intention."

She frowned as she considered the viability of his request. "Very well," she said. "I still have to do some routine investigation of your situation. It would help if you'd provide references, both financial and personal."

"Done. Will that take care of it?"

"Not quite. *If* you can get a letter of consent from the mother, a copy of the baby's birth certificate and a medical-permission slip in my hands by the end of the day, then I'll recommend that Toni be returned to you."

"Returned tonight?"

She smiled. "I'll do my best. If she is, a case manager will be assigned to check up on you. You realize that even when Ms. Donati returns this won't be over, don't you? In the eyes of the law, she abandoned her child. We take a very dim view of that."

"She'll have the support of the Salvatore family. And she'll have her husband's support."

"I hope, for her sake, you're right."

A few minutes later, Ms. Cartwright left and Luc grabbed Grace, wrapping his arms about her waist and twirling her around until the room spun in a dizzy arc.

"We did it!" he announced jubilantly, setting her back on her feet. "Didn't I tell you everything would work out?"

"Yes, you did," Grace murmured, clutching his shoulders.

But she wasn't quite as confident. Not only were their lies compounding by the hour, so was her commitment to Luc and the baby. How could she possibly face Dom and claim she'd kept her part of the bargain, when she'd become so involved in this situation with Toni.... Toni? What about Luc? She closed her eyes. If she was honest—and she had to concede that honesty was something in disastrously short supply these days—she'd admit she'd become very involved with Luc.

If she didn't get out of this situation soon, she'd lose everything... Baby Dream Toys, for one. But far worse, her heart.

CHAPTER EIGHT

The Great Lie
Day 340 and complications abound...

TONI ARRIVED SAFELY back at Luc's apartment by dinner time that evening and all Luc's brothers were there to celebrate her return. Dinner proved to be loud and rowdy, not that Toni seemed bothered by the noise and confusion. If anything, she reveled in it. Wearing a frilly pink dress and a matching bow, she charmed one uncle after another with her full repertoire of baby coos, babbles and toothless grins. It wasn't until the gathering started to break up that the trouble began.

"This is an interesting addition," Marc proclaimed loudly. He snatched Grace's hand and examined the wedding band decorating her finger. In ten seconds flat, Luc's brothers had her surrounded.

"Is it real?" Stef demanded.

"You didn't marry that Will-William guy, did you?" Alessandro questioned in a disapproving voice. "He's not good enough for you, Grace—not if he makes you dress like a bag lady."

Before Grace could answer, Luc cut through and snagged her elbow. "The wedding band is there because I put it on her finger," he announced, tucking her close to his side.

Dead silence met his explanation. Then Rocco asked, "But is it real?"

For a moment Grace thought Luc would lie. She poked her elbow in his side to discourage any such plan. "Don't you dare," she muttered. "I've had my fill of fibs."

He stared down at her, his eyes glittering with devilry. Shrugging, he admitted, "No. It's not real."

"Yet?" Marc suggested with a grin.

Luc ignored him. "The people at social services believe it is real. If anyone finds out otherwise, we'll lose Toni. So keep your mouths shut."

Stef's face was a study in confusion. "When did this marriage business start? I thought you guys were just pretending to be engaged."

"That's for the police. Get with it, bro," Alessandro said with an exasperated sigh. "Look..." He ticked off on his fingers. "They're boss and assistant at work, engaged for the police, married for the baby people and just good friends in front of us."

"You guys ever consider scorecards? This is getting confusing," Stef complained.

Alessandro lifted an eyebrow, his expression reminding Grace forcefully of Luc. "What I want to know is which category they fall into when they're alone with Toni."

"Maybe they don't fall into any category," Marc suggested with a mock leer in Grace's direction. "Maybe they fall into the nearest bed."

"That's enough," Luc said, a hint of anger sparking in his eyes.

"Yeah!" Rocco slugged Marc in the arm. "Watch your mouth."

"I'd rather watch Grace's."

"Oh, yeah? How are you going to do that with two black eyes?"

Marc's hands balled into fists. "You'll have to land a punch first—something you haven't been able to do since I was twelve."

"Then, it's about time I remedied that oversight!"

"Do it, Rocco," Stef cheered him on. "This I gotta see."

"I said, that's enough!" Luc glared from one to the other. "Get out of here, the lot of you. Toni's just been put to bed and I won't have you waking her up again. We get little enough sleep as it is."

"That answers that question," Marc said with a hoot. "Maybe you'd get more rest if you didn't spend your nights jumping Grace's—"

Luc silenced his brother with a single look. "Time to go. All of you, out of here," he said, maneuvering them from the room and out the front door. This time, they didn't make a sound as they left, though Marc thumbed his nose at Mrs. Bumgartle's door before anyone could restrain him.

Alone again with Luc, Grace glanced at him with a troubled expression. "Is it really wise to involve your brothers in this deception? I feel guilty enough, as it is."

"Really? Did you feel guilty pretending to be engaged to William?" he asked, crossing to stand in front of her.

She looked away, hot color creeping into her cheeks. "That was different."

He hooked her chin with his finger and forced her to look at him. "Was it? Why?"

"You know why. I wasn't trying to deceive the police or social services."

"No, only me." His watchful gaze sharpened. "You never did explain that."

She stepped away from him. To her relief, he let her go. "Didn't I?" she asked evasively.

"No. Care to take a stab at it now?"

"Not really."

"Afraid?" he mocked. "Shall I guess why you did it?"

"We've already played this game, Luc?" She spoke more sharply than she'd intended. "It didn't end well."

"Did I win? I can't seem to remember."

"I believe it was a draw."

"Then, I insist on a rematch."

Not since their deception began, had she felt this vulnerable. Her attraction to Luc grew with each passing moment they spent together, as did her craving for his touch, his kisses, his passion. How, after holding him at a distance for eleven long months, could she now be on the verge of surrendering?

Catching her by the elbows, he tugged her close. He looked so large and enticing. She rested her hands on his chest, feeling the hard muscles tauten beneath her fingertips. It took every ounce of determination not to let her hands roam, exploring what lay beneath his crisp white shirt.

She bowed her head, fighting her wayward urges. "Luc, don't," she whispered.

"I think you disguised your appearance and wore that engagement ring for protection."

"Protection?" She managed a light laugh. "That's nonsense."

He shook his head, eyeing her with a nerve-racking intensity. "No. I think I'm right. My guess is you had a bad experience with your last employer." His voice held a tender note that completely disarmed her. "Did he harass you? Is that why you went to such lengths to protect yourself—because you thought I might be like him? I can understand, sympathize even. But why let the pretence go on for so long, once you knew I wasn't like that?''

She felt like a worm. He'd gotten the wrong end of the stick entirely. How could she tell him that far from such a reasonable, sympathetic motivation, she'd gone to such lengths because of his father's request and her own greed. ''No! You're wrong, Luc. I swear it.''

He lifted an eyebrow, a teasing smile tugging at his mouth. ''After all the deception between us, I'm supposed to believe you?''

If he only knew! ''For your information, until I started working at Salvatore's I'd told a grand total of six lies in my entire life.''

He slid a hand along the nape of her neck, his fingers sinking into her hair. ''Then I'll assume you've been making up for lost time.''

She stirred within his hold. ''You promised not to touch me, remember?''

''I remember.'' His mouth hovered a breath away from hers. ''But it was a promise meant to be broken.''

His head came down and his kiss blocked all thought, all resistance. She slid her arms around his waist, desire racing like wildfire, threatening to flare out of control. He pressed her close, his thighs cradling hers, and she snuggled into his embrace, the feelings he aroused unlike any she'd ever experienced.

Drawing back slightly, he loosened the top few buttons of her blouse. Sweeping it from her shoulders, he exposed the long line of her neck and sloping curves of her breasts. He lowered his head, pressing a lingering kiss in the soft hollow of her throat.

''I want you, *mia amorata*,'' he muttered, his breath fast and hot against her neck.

Her heart pounded beneath his hands and she shook her head, desperately clinging to the tiny bit of sanity remaining to her. Every instinct urged her to give in to his demands, but she couldn't cross that line, couldn't permit a physical relationship without the emotional commitment to go with it. "We can't. It wouldn't be right." But it felt right—exquisitely right.

"It would be wrong not to," he argued. "What's the problem? You've admitted there's no William. Your job is safe. You want me. And I want you."

His hands tightened on her hips, making the extent of his desire abundantly clear. She wasn't certain how much longer she could hold him off. She wasn't certain how much longer she *wanted* to hold him off. But she had to try. "Luc, this is crazy. We've known each other for almost a year and this has never happened. Think about it. We're under a lot of stress. We're forced to live together in very difficult circumstances. It's...it's an involuntary reaction or something."

He stared at her in disbelief. "An involuntary reaction? You're kidding, right?"

"I'm serious," she insisted. "It's the situation we're in, it's not because we really want...you know."

He laughed, the sound harsh and taunting. "Believe me when I say that I really want...you know. I ache for...you know. If I don't experience...you know soon, I might do something drastic—like bite the damned buttons right off your blouse."

"Luc!"

"You don't get it, do you? I want to kiss every inch of your body, starting with that luscious mouth of yours. I want to strip off your clothes and make long, sweet love to you. And I want to do it in every room of this apartment, starting right here and now. And once we've done that, I'll want to do it all over again. Does that give you some idea of how much I want...you know?''

She wondered if she looked as shocked as she felt. Nervously, she licked her lips and watched in fascination as Luc's eyes flared a brilliant gold. ''Where is this leading?'' she asked.

''Straight to bed,'' he answered without missing a beat.

''That's not what I mean, and you know it. Are you interested in marriage, or are we just talking about an affair?''

His hands tightened on her shoulders. ''You'd like an honest answer, I assume?''

''It would be refreshing.''

He hesitated, then said bluntly, ''I want to make love to you. That's as honest as I can be at this point.''

''I see.''

She looked away, hoping to hide her distress. He'd been very tactful. But the bottom line was, he wanted a mistress, not a wife. It wasn't as if she hadn't suspected as much. Still, she hadn't anticipated how badly the truth would hurt. Stepping from his hold, she pulled the front of her blouse closed. She didn't try to button it. Her hands were trembling too much to even try.

''Grace...''

''What about my job? I mean, affairs don't last forever. An ending is inevitable.''

''Whether we decide to become involved or not, I don't think we should work together any longer,'' he said carefully. ''There's an opening at management level. I'd planned to tell you about it at your year-end review. It would mean a promotion—more money, great potential for advancement.''

She could hardly take it all in. She'd never suspected he might want to promote her. Nor could she deny how tempted she was by his offer. Too tempted. She had to remember Baby Dream Toys. Only, why had remembering become such a struggle? Wrapping her arms around her waist, she said, "This is too much, too soon. I need time. I'd rather not do anything I'll later regret while we're still taking care of Toni."

"You want to wait until Pietro and Carina return, is that it?"

"Yes."

"That won't be for another week. Not until Thanksgiving."

Her head jerked up and she stared at him. "What!"

"I'm sorry. I should have told you sooner." He watched her with a hooded expression. "I guess I had other things on my mind. Pietro called right before my brothers arrived. They're still in Italy with Carina's family, while her mother recuperates. He says Carina's talking to him now, but he hasn't convinced her to marry him yet."

"But seven more days! When does Dom get back?" she asked in a panic.

"He's due in the week after Thanksgiving."

That cut it close. Too close. She needed time to think, to get her priorities straight. Whether he realized it or not, Luc was asking her to sacrifice everything she'd worked so hard to attain. And for what? A brief affair. A few weeks or months of passion. How could she agree to that? Her answer should be obvious. And it would be, if it weren't for one small detail. She wanted him every bit as much as he wanted her.

"Grace?"

"I need time," she informed him. She fought to cloak herself in the calm, collected air she'd spent eleven long months cultivating. It was more of a struggle than she would have thought possible. Where had her control gone? Her detachment? "Once our lives get back to normal, I'll give you my answer."

"By Thanksgiving?"

After a brief hesitation, she nodded. "By Thanksgiving."

"And between now and then?"

The look she cast him was direct. "You're not to touch me. Not a kiss. Not so much as a hug. I don't intend to be seduced into a decision."

She could tell he wasn't pleased. "And if I don't agree?"

"Then you can explain to social services why your wife doesn't live with you." Not waiting for his reaction to her threat—not allowing herself time to change her mind and tumble back into his arms—she practically ran from the room.

THE NEXT FIVE DAYS proved to be the longest of Grace's life. Now, a mere forty-eight hours from their Thanksgiving deadline, the final days of her tenure at Salvatore's crept ever closer, as did the day of Dom's return. True to his word, Luc didn't lay a finger on her, which stretched both their frustration levels to the limits. As a result, she didn't know whether to thank him for keeping his promise or hit him. But since she'd been the one to set the rules, she was stuck with them.

How she wished she'd had the chance to talk to her father—to get his help and advice. But they'd been out of touch for the past couple of weeks, and though she'd left messages, they kept missing each other.

The doorbell rang. "Luc!" Grace called, struggling to pin the diaper around Toni—a determinedly wiggly Toni.

"Get the door. It's probably the case manager. Can you answer it?"

"What?"

"The doorbell!"

"I'll get it."

Grace sighed, snapping and buttoning as quickly as she could. "You don't give your uncle this much trouble when *he* changes you. I think it's very unfair of you to fight me, since I'm the one who just filled you up with a nice, warm bottle."

Toni responded with a string of bubbles and a determined pumping of limbs. Just as Grace finished, she heard the front door crash shut. An instant later, Luc raced into the room. One look warned her it was bad news.

"Quick!" he said, snatching Toni off the changing table and dumping her into a laundry basket of clean baby clothes that was sitting on the bed. "Come with me. Hurry."

"You can't put Toni in there! Luc! What's wrong? What's happening?"

He didn't answer, simply clutched the basket and dashed toward his bedroom. Grace gave chase. The doorbell rang again, a strident, urgent sound. Flinging open his louvered closet doors, Luc swept shoes to one side and set the laundry basket on the floor. Toni gurgled happily. Propelling Grace in beside the basket, he slammed the door.

"Stay there," he ordered. "Don't move and don't make any noise."

"Luc!" She thrust the door open and poked her head out. *"What is going on?"*

"In case you weren't aware of it, when you open your mouth and speak, you make noise. You've got to be *quiet!*" The doorbell rang again, short, multiple, staccato rings. Kissing her swiftly, Luc pushed her toward the back of the huge closet. "My dad's here. Now keep it down." He closed the door.

Grace opened the door. "Dom's here?" she asked in a panicked whisper. "He's not due back for another week."

"I don't have time for this," he said through gritted teeth. "Dad can't find out about Toni until Pietro and Carina are married or he'll disown the lot of them. Which means you two have to stay hidden."

"I understand that. But why here? Why not the guest room?"

He ran an impatient hand through his hair. "This is the safest place in the house. He hasn't been in my bedroom since the time he walked in without knocking and caught the cleaning lady making my bed. So you should be fine *if* you keep quiet." He slammed the door shut.

She opened it, staring at him in bewilderment. "What was wrong with the cleaning lady making your bed?"

He spared her a brief grin. "She was naked at the time." The doorbell was ringing nonstop now. "Grace, for crying out loud! Open this door again and I'll haul you out there, introduce you as my wife and tell him Toni is yours!"

Without another word, she slammed the door shut. To her disbelief, Toni had fallen asleep. How could Toni possibly nap through all the confusion? Grace wondered in amazement. Babies were such strange, little creatures. She heard the front door crash again. Had Dom left already? Did she dare sneak out and see?

Infuriated Italian burst from the direction of the living room. Well, that answered that question. Unable to resist, she pressed her ear to the louvered slats. Dom was still speaking... or yelling... in Italian.

"I told you I was sorry," she heard Luc's deep voice reply in English. He sounded remarkably calm. "Why didn't you let us know you were coming?"

"I wished to surprise you for Thanksgiving. I called the office. They said you were working from your apartment. Why is this?"

"It seemed like a good idea at the time," came the dry reply.

There was a long silence, and Grace could almost see Dom mull over Luc's response. "You have a woman here, am I right?" he demanded. "That is why you slam the door in my face. Where have you hidden her?"

Grace shrank back, tripped, and tumbled to the floor next to the laundry basket. She gripped her fingers together and prayed they hadn't heard her—praying even harder that Toni wouldn't wake up and bellow in annoyance.

"Actually, I have two," came Luc's cool response. "A blonde and a brunette."

Grace held her breath, waiting for Dom's reaction— waiting for him to explode or come and ferret her from her hiding place. An instant later she heard his bark of laughter. "*Due.* That is a good one. I almost believe you."

"You want to check the bedroom? I have them hiding in there."

It was all Grace could do to keep from shrieking. Was he crazy? Luc's question seemed to hang in the air for endless minutes. Then Dom sighed. "I apologized for that little incident," he grumbled. "The young lady forgave me, even if you did not. I wish to change the subject. Where is Grace? I asked for her at the office and they said she was out as well.''

"I gave her the afternoon off. She's been working very hard lately.''

"She is a good girl. I am very fond of her.''

"There's certainly more to her than meets the eye.''

Dom chuckled. "I think your words are more true than you realize.''

"Don't count on it," came Luc's risky reply. "But enough about business. How was your trip to Italy? We've missed you.''

As their voices grew fainter, dropping to a gentle rumble, Grace curled up next to the laundry basket. That had been close. If Dom had walked in and discovered her... She shuddered. It would have meant the end of her plan to open Baby Dream Toys.

Not that it didn't anyway.

She dropped her chin to her knees and sighed. One thing she did know—she couldn't avoid Dom forever. What would she say when they met? She couldn't very well pretend this year had gone off without a hitch. She'd have to be honest with him, tell him what she'd been up to the past ten or eleven days.

If he chose to renege on their deal, she wouldn't argue. After all, she'd been the one to break their agreement. Remembering Luc's passionate kisses with a wistful longing, she was forced to admit she'd broken the agreement more than just a time or two. Once in possession of all the facts, Dom would be within his rights to refuse to set her up in business. Well, she could live with that.

But what about Luc...? She bit her lip. She didn't doubt he'd find out the real reason for her disguise, discover that her motives had been less than pure. It was inevitable that Dom would tell Luc the truth. How would he react when he found out? She closed her eyes, stifling a groan. She knew how he'd react. Those gorgeous golden eyes of his would ice up. Her job as his assistant would be over. Her management-position job offer would vanish like dust in a high wind. And their affair would end before it ever began. Just as it should.

She fought back a sob, smothering the sound against her knees. Time to face facts. Because the fact was that at some point she'd fallen hopelessly, helplessly in love with Luc Salvatore. And as much as she should care about the loss of Baby Dream Toys, she cared more about losing Luc.

Sitting there on the closet floor—alone and hurting—she faced the death of all her dreams. And no matter how hard she tried, she couldn't prevent a scalding tear from drifting down her cheek.

LUC SURREPTITIOUSLY checked his watch as he escorted Dom to the door. "It's great having you home, Dad. Thanks for dropping by."

"It is very good to be home. I decided to return early so I could have the whole family over for Thanksgiving dinner." He paused in the entranceway. "Would this be convenient?"

"Terrific. Just terrific." Luc opened the door.

A young woman dressed in a business suit, with wire-rimmed glasses perched on the end of her nose, stood there, poised to knock. "Oh, my goodness," she exclaimed. "You startled me." Recovering swiftly, she held out her hand. "Hello. I'm Miss Carstairs," she announced. "I'm your—"

"My masseuse!" Luc greeted her loudly. Grabbing her hand, he yanked her into the apartment. "At last!"

"No! I—"

Dom chuckled. "A blonde, a brunette and now a red-head." He wagged his finger at Luc. "I knew you were up to no good. One of these days, my boy..."

Luc wrapped an arm around the shocked social worker. "I never could put one over on you. Talk to you later, Dad, and welcome home." He slammed the door closed.

Miss Carstairs wriggled from his hold, stumbling back against the door. "Oh, my," she murmured, red-faced and breathless. She tucked a stray curl back into the tight knot on top of her head. "I am *not* the masseuse!"

Luc lifted an eyebrow. "You're not?"

"No! I'm Miss Carstairs, from social services. Are you Mr. Salvatore?"

"In the flesh. Pleased to meet you." He offered his hand.

She stared at his outstretched fingers as if they had fangs and a rattle. "I'm... I'm your case manager." She peered up at him suspiciously. "Are you sure you're Luc Salvatore? Mr. Luc Salvatore, whose wife is Mrs. Grace Salvatore?"

"That's right."

Perhaps he shouldn't have introduced her as his masseuse, but it was the only thing he could think of at the time. If he was smart, he'd get little Miss Carstairs on her way fast—before she discovered Grace and Toni hiding in the closet. Social services would have the baby out of his apartment like a shot if that happened.

"Listen, I'm sorry but Grace and Toni aren't in." Dropping his hands to her shoulders, he peeled her off the door, opened it and glanced up and down the hallway. Dom was nowhere in sight. "How about coming back tomorrow?'' Planting his hand in the small of her back, he propelled her into the hall.

A loud baby bellow resounded through the apartment and Miss Carstairs's eyebrows flew up. ''Your wife and Antonia are out? And what, may I ask, is that crying? It certainly sounds like a baby to me.''

Before he could stop her, she charged back into the apartment, leaving him no choice but to give chase. Following the sound of a very cranky Toni, she hustled into his bedroom and hesitated in front of the closet. Shooting him a look of disbelief, she threw open the closet door.

Luc inhaled sharply, positive he'd never seen a more appealing sight in his life. Grace sat there on the floor, Toni clutched to her breast. Wispy golden curls framed her sleep-flushed face. She blinked up at them, her light green eyes soft and drowsy. Clearly, she'd just woken up.

''You make your wife and niece live in a closet?'' Miss Carstairs demanded, turning on him. ''Or do you just make them sleep in there.''

''No, I don't make my wife and niece live in a closet,'' Luc stated forcefully. ''Nor do they sleep there. Most days. My father... You see, Grace...'' He shoved his hand through his hair and sighed in exasperation. ''It's a long story.''

Miss Carstairs folded her arms across her chest and tapped her foot. ''I have all the time in the world.''

Slipping Toni back into the laundry basket, Grace crawled out of the closet. Attempting to stand proved more difficult. Her knees buckled. Luc caught her. ''My legs fell asleep,'' she murmured apologetically. ''How long was your father here?''

''Ninety long, impossible minutes,'' he replied, cradling her close until she could shake the pins and needles from her legs. He gazed down into her face and frowned. Cupping her chin, he ran his thumb across her cheekbone, a question in his eyes. "*Cara?* Are you all right?" he asked in a low voice.

A hint of color lit Grace's face. Could he tell she'd been crying? Lord, she hoped not. She shifted her attention to the social worker, offering a smile and a hand. "Hi. I'm Grace...Salvatore."

"Lillian Carstairs. May I ask if you and the baby often hide in your husband's closet?"

"It's the first time that I'm aware of," Luc answered for Grace. "I can't vouch for any other closets, however. Have you hidden in any others?"

"Only one. When I was twelve."

"Excuse me," Miss Carstairs interrupted. "Let's just deal with this closet and this time. Why were you hiding in the closet?"

"So Dom—Luc's father—wouldn't find us," Grace answered.

Luc released a gusty sigh. "My father doesn't know about Toni. For that matter, he doesn't know that Grace and I are married. We...eloped while he was still in Italy. And until I tell him..."

"Your wife and niece will be kept hidden away in the closet?" the social worker suggested dryly.

"We'll use the bathroom next time," Grace offered. "Would that be all right?"

"Perhaps it would be best if you told him the truth," Miss Carstairs said in no uncertain terms. "I suppose that also explains the rather...unusual greeting at the door."

A hint of amusement lightened Luc's expression. "I'm sorry. I didn't want to introduce you to my father. He'd already assumed the worst as far as your presence was concerned, and I just went along with it. I apologize, if I offended you.''

Color spotted Miss Carstairs's cheeks and Grace could tell that the infamous Salvatore charm was working its magic once more. "This is all highly irregular," the young woman muttered.

"How about if we start over," Luc suggested. "Come on into the kitchen and have a cup of coffee, and then we'll show you around and answer any questions you might have. Coffee, Grace?''

"Sounds great," she agreed.

"And a bottle for Toni, I think."

Grace pulled the basket from the closet and picked up Toni. Once again Luc would talk his way out of a sticky situation. How she wished she had his gift. It would certainly come in handy over the next few days.

She closed her eyes and buried her face against Toni's neck. Matters were becoming much too complicated. How much longer could she keep doing this—living a lie? Perhaps she'd better confess her subterfuge to Luc once Miss Carstairs left. She'd be as frank with him as she intended to be with Dom. But if she did, how would Luc react? Would he understand why she'd chosen to deceive him? Somehow, she suspected he wouldn't. At the very least, it would change their relationship, and she didn't think she was ready for that.

"Grace?" Luc called to her. "Are you coming?"

She lifted her head and took a deep breath. Maybe she'd have a hot cup of coffee and think about it for a while. There was no rush, right? She'd get a good night's sleep and reconsider her options tomorrow.

Though, somehow, she suspected matters wouldn't be any more clear-cut come morning.

CHAPTER NINE

The Great Lie
Day 346 and Grace's situation can't get any darker... or can it...?

AS SHE SUSPECTED, having a night to sleep on her problems brought Grace no nearer a solution. If anything, she awoke more confused than ever. She had several choices, none quite what she wanted. She buried her head in the pillow with a groan. Should she tell Luc about her deal with Dom? Should she accept his very tempting offer of a promotion, if she was unable to open Baby Dream Toys? Most important of all, should she agree to a temporary relationship and suffer the resulting consequences.

She didn't know. She just didn't know. What she wanted was Luc. But Luc didn't want her, at least not on a permanent basis. And facing that fact nearly ripped her apart.

Crawling out of bed to a brilliant, sunny morning, she discovered Luc already up and dressed in a business suit and tie.

"You're not going into the office, are you?" she asked, dismayed. She'd hoped to spend time with him—precious, fleeting time.

"I'm afraid so. Dad said he'd meet me there. I assume he'd like an update on our various business activities.

And since the only other option is to have him come here..." He let the suggestion hang.

"No, that wouldn't work, would it," she agreed. "What about Pietro and Carina?"

"I still expect them tomorrow for Thanksgiving. If they weren't going to make it, Pietro would have phoned. Will you stay here with Toni? If Dad asks, I'll say you're out sick."

"More lies," she murmured, disheartened.

He frowned, then approached and pulled her into his arms. "I know this is difficult for you. But we can straighten everything out when Pietro returns. How about once this is over, we confess our various sins? You and I will have a frank talk and put all our cards on the table."

She smiled. "I'd like that. And you're right, of course. I have a sin or two of my own to confess."

"Somehow that doesn't surprise me." He dropped a kiss on her mouth. Then, as if unable to resist, he kissed her again, more deeply, with an underlying urgency. "Grace...I know I'm breaking our agreement, but I can't help it. I want you."

She nestled into his embrace, and suddenly everything crystallized in her mind. Through the long, endless night, she'd struggled to make a decision. To decide whether she'd fight for Luc's love or do the safe thing and walk away. But now, in the cold light of day, she knew what her answer would be. In that instant, held in his arms, all her doubts vanished.

For the first time since their escapade began, she was certain in both heart and mind. Once they'd settled their problems with Toni, she'd tell Luc the truth. Every bit of it. Then, it would be up to him how they proceeded. She knew he wasn't interested in a permanent relationship, and though it meant future heartache, she'd take the tiny slice of heaven he offered. Because she knew, deep in her heart, that she'd never love anyone as much as she loved Luc.

"I want you, too," she admitted. And though she wished she could tell him of her love, that she could coax similar words from him, she was willing to give it time. Maybe even a lifetime.

His eyes darkened. "Say that again."

"I want you," she repeated. "Very, very badly."

"You sure that isn't frustration speaking?" he asked, skepticism clear in his voice. "What about when Toni's out of our life and you've had time to reconsider? What will you say then?"

"The same."

She'd surprised him, and he studied her expression intently. "You're sure?"

"I'm positive," she said, and he couldn't mistake her sincerity.

"Just so you know, your timing *really* stinks," he told her with a short, impatient laugh. Pulling her more fully into his arms, he kissed her again, the embrace passionate and thorough. "As much as I want to carry you back to bed, I have to leave."

"Will you be gone all day?" she asked wistfully. "Can you break off early?"

"I hope so. I'll see if I can't return for lunch." And with a final kiss, he left.

She secured the door behind him and leaned her forehead against the cool wooden surface. Another day or two and her subterfuge would end. Pietro would return, Toni would be back with her parents, and she and Luc would clear up all the lies and deceptions between them. She could hang on for that long, couldn't she? Not that she had a choice. Straightening, she tightened the sash on her robe and padded toward the guest bedroom. Toni lay in her crib, watching the mobile spin lazily above her.

"Good morning," Grace said with a smile. "You're certainly in a happy mood this morning. Ready for breakfast? Or should we have our bath first." Toni kicked her feet and let out a shrill gurgle. "Breakfast, it is."

Lifting the baby out of the crib, Grace headed for the kitchen, when a peremptory knock sounded at the door. Later, she realized she should have peered through the spy hole first. But at the time, she didn't think twice. She opened the door.

Dom Salvatore stood there.

He looked at her, took a stumbling step backward, double-checked the number on the door and then looked at her once more. Slowly his gaze took in her sleep-ruffled hair—her sleep-ruffled *blond* hair, her bathrobe-covered nightie, and finally the baby Grace held clutched in her arms. His face crumpled.

"You are not wearing your glasses," he blurted.

"No," she confessed. "I'm not."

"And your hair..."

"I know. It's blond again." She touched the tangled curls self-consciously, then stepped back. "Why don't you come in."

He looked appalled, and for an instant she thought he'd burst into tears. Then he slowly followed her into the apartment. "All my plans...ruined," he moaned.

"It's not so bad," she attempted to reassure him, wondering desperately which story to tell. Did she mention Pietro and Carina? Did she claim Toni as her own? Lord, how she wished Luc was here to help.

Dom shook his head, muttering in Italian. Finally, he implored, "How could this happen?"

Oh, Lord. How should she answer? She had to pick a story and fast, and salvage what she could of this mess. She bit down on her lip, forced to face facts with a vengeance. It was too late to save herself, but... She straightened her shoulders. She could still help Pietro and Carina.

To her relief, Toni came to the rescue. Reacting to the heightened emotions, her face screwed into a frown and she began to cry. "Oh, dear," Grace said, "I think we'd better get busy with that bottle."

"Please wait." For a long minute Dom stared at Toni, uncertainty clouding his face. Grace could see his quandary, his delight at the possibility of a grandchild warring with his outrage at the circumstances behind that grandchild's conception. Then his hands inched out and he took the wailing baby into his arms. He jiggled Toni gently and when she stopped crying, he beamed. "And who have we here?"

"This is your granddaughter, Antonia," Grace said simply.

A look of wonder dawned on his face. "A granddaughter," he murmured in astonishment. "But... this is marvelous. How old is she?"

Grace's gaze slipped away from his. "Three months."

He gaped at Grace. "Three..." He burst into volatile Italian, stabbing the air with his free hand. She didn't understand a single word he spoke, but she knew exactly what he said. In order for her to have given birth to Toni, she would have had to tumble into Luc's bed her first day on the job. At long last, he drew breath. *"Three months!"* he exclaimed.

What possible explanation could she give that would appease him? "The disguise didn't work," she said, her face burning with humiliation.

"This I have figured out for myself!"

To her relief, Toni once again came to her rescue. Wriggling in her grandfather's arms she began to fuss. "She's hungry," Grace said. "I need to feed her." Leading the way into the kitchen, she popped a bottle into the microwave. "Would you like a cup of coffee?"

"That would be very kind of you." He sat down at the kitchen table, holding Toni on his lap. "Tell me, Grace. What happened?"

She cleared her throat, pouring the fragrant brew into a cup. "Well . . . It's a long story." To her relief, the microwave beeped, providing her with a few extra seconds to gather her thoughts. "Would you like to give Toni her bottle?"

"I'd be honored." He cradled his granddaughter in the crook of his arm and Toni stared up at him with wide, curious eyes. Dom offered her the nipple and without hesitation she took it, wrapping her tiny fingers around Dom's and sucking contentedly. He glanced at Grace with a bittersweet smile. "She is the image of my own Anna. Thank you for naming her after her grandmother. It touches me deeply."

"She's a good baby," Grace said gently, unwilling to take credit for something that had nothing to do with her.

"A beautiful baby. You have done a wonderful job, my dear." Then he fixed her with a stern gaze. "And now, you will tell me your story, please. You say the disguise did not work? Not even for a single day?"

"Not really." She poured a second cup of coffee and took a sip. "Luc's not an easy man to fool."

Dom clicked his tongue. "But a girl with such an impeccable background. Could you not resist him?"

"He's hard to resist," she confessed.

"But still..." He seemed to be searching for a reasonable explanation. "I thought starting your own business was important to you. I thought that, if nothing else, such an agreement would keep you from my son's arms." He shook his head and released a deep, heartfelt sigh. "You must love Luciano very much, to give up your dream."

To her dismay, tears welled in her eyes. "Starting Baby Dream Toys meant more to me than anything. I wanted to keep our agreement. I really did. Please believe that I tried. I wore the disguise and pretended to be engaged. But, Luc... He... I..." Her throat closed over and helplessly, she bowed her head.

"I am sorry, my dear. I did not mean to upset you." He stroked Toni's head with a gentle hand. Then, he looked up, pinning her with a reluctant, though stern gaze. "I must tell you I am very disappointed in you both. It is my deepest hope that you and Luc have taken proper responsibility for your unthinking actions. As much as this grandchild means to me, as much as my son means to me, I would throw you out of the family if I thought you had not." He paused, waiting for her response.

Grace swallowed, realizing she was treading on very shaky ground. "You'd throw us out of the family if we hadn't... what?" she asked hesitantly.

"Married, of course! You are wed, yes?"

A footstep sounded behind her. And then, "Of course, we're married, Dad," Luc announced from the doorway.

Grace spun around, her eyes widening in horror. Without any question, he'd overheard every word of their conversation. And he was *furious*. His eyes glittered with harsh gold lights and he stalked into the kitchen, reminding her of an angry panther she'd once seen pacing his cage at the zoo, roaring his frustration to the heavens. She tensed, waiting for Luc's roar.

"What are you doing here, Dad?" To her surprise, he spoke in a deceptively mild voice. But one glimpse of his set features warned her that, though he wouldn't lose his temper in front of his father, he wouldn't be so restrained when he got her alone. "I thought we agreed to meet at the office."

"So we did," Dom agreed, not seeming to notice anything amiss. He set the bottle on the table and lifted Toni to his shoulder, patting her back. "It occurred to me we might drive into work together." He fixed his calm, dark gaze on Luc. "You forgot to tell me something yesterday, yes?"

Luc shrugged, pouring himself a cup of coffee. "As I recall, I did mention I had a blonde and brunette hiding in my bedroom."

"I thought you made a joke," Dom dismissed contemptuously. "You know this. Why did you not tell me the truth? You marry, have a child, and do not bother to tell your own father?" He added something in Italian, hurt clear in his lilting voice.

Luc hesitated, then asked, "If I had told you, what would you have done?"

"I would have come home," came the prompt response.

"There's your answer. The doctors wanted you to retire. You know you wouldn't have, if you'd returned early from Italy."

"Bah! Doctors. What do they know? I am strong as a horse."

"A sixty-five-year-old horse with a heart condition."

Dom stirred uncomfortably. "I wish to talk about Grace and this situation we now find ourselves in, not about my health. You uncovered the truth about her, I am right?"

Luc leaned back against the counter and sipped his coffee. For a split second his gaze locked with hers. She froze, held in place by the icy fury she read there. "Uncovered the truth about her disguise and the fake engagement? Yes. I uncovered that much." But not about his father's bribe. Grace caught the omission. Not about his starting her up in business.

And Luc's expression warned he wouldn't easily forgive that exclusion.

Betraying his nervousness, Dom ran a hand along his jaw. "You...ah...you are not upset with me?"

"Should I be?"

Dom stiffened. "Is this why you did not tell me about Antonia? You were angered that we deceived you?"

Luc's expression softened. "*No, Papa.* I wouldn't do that. I've explained why I didn't notify you. You needed to get away from Salvatore Enterprises. This past year has allowed you time to recuperate and me time to take control of the business."

"Then, it was good I hired Grace. She has helped you focus on your work."

Grace winced, waiting for Luc's tenuous control of his temper finally to snap. "You didn't need to involve someone else," Luc bit out, slamming his coffee mug to the counter. "You should have trusted me to take care of the work situation without interfering."

"Perhaps." Dom shrugged, not in the least intimidated by his son's wrath. "But I wished to insure you would have a full year to concentrate on work and not be subjected to...irresistible temptations." He glanced at Grace and smiled apologetically. "This will not be a problem anymore, eh? Once a Salvatore falls in love and marries, it is for life. The eyes, they become blind to every other woman."

It was all Grace could do not to weep. How she wanted that to be true. But as much as she might wish it otherwise, Luc hadn't fallen in love with her, merely in lust. And that minor detail ensured a broken heart at the end of their affair. Assuming they even had an affair. In the meantime, she couldn't continue to stand there quietly as though condoning any further lies. Rinsing her coffee cup at the sink, she crossed to where Dom sat.

"Would you excuse us?" she murmured, scooping Toni into her arms. "I think it's time we got dressed."

Dom stood. "I am happy I returned for Thanksgiving," he said, enfolding her in a tender embrace and kissing her cheeks. "I have come home to find much to be grateful for."

Unable to think of a single response, Grace offered a watery smile. Turning to leave the room, she shot Luc a swift, beseeching look, praying he'd understand her silent plea. Perhaps agreeing to Dom's plan had been wrong, but it had been the offer of a lifetime—too good to refuse. Would Luc understand that? Would he at least be willing to listen to her explanation?

Twenty minutes later Grace returned with Toni, in time to bid Dom farewell. She stood next to Luc and smiled calmly, striving to appear the perfect wife. The minute his father disappeared down the hallway, Luc turned on her.

"Every damned word out of your mouth has been a lie, hasn't it?" he snarled, kicking the door shut. It bounced back ajar, but he ignored it, stalking after her.

"Not every word." She backed toward the living room, clutching Toni to her breast like a shield. Realizing she couldn't continue to hide behind a baby, she spread a blanket on the floor and set Toni on it. Then she turned to face Luc. "Besides," she said, refusing to be intimidated by his fury. "What about all *your* lies?"

"I lied to protect the baby," he was quick to defend. "They were necessary lies."

She lifted her chin. "They're still lies. As far as protecting the baby... Haven't I done everything possible to help you since Toni arrived? Haven't I lied to the police and to the social-service people, in order to cover for Pietro and Carina? And for what? For you! What more do you want from me? I even lied to your father. And that cost me the chance to start my own business."

Her words brought home the cold, hard facts and she stared at him with anguished eyes, the full extent of her predicament finally sinking in. "My own business," she whispered. To her horror, she burst into tears. She looked around helplessly, trying to remember where the tissues were kept.

"Here."

He held out a handkerchief and she took it gratefully, struggling to stem the flood of tears. "I'm sorry," she managed to say. "It must be the stress."

Luc thrust his hands into his trouser pockets, a muscle leaping in his jaw. "Explain it to me. The deal you had with Dad."

She waved the damp hanky. "You already know most of it."

He paced in front of her. "I sure as hell didn't know you were in cahoots with my father."

"That's the only fact you didn't have. You knew about the disguise, the fake engagement . . ."

He nailed her with a disbelieving look. "And my *father* put you up to it?"

Reluctantly, she nodded. "He seemed to think it was the only way he could retire. All your employees kept falling in love with you and making a mess of the office situation. He thought I'd be different."

"Why?"

She shrugged. "He thought I'd be more levelheaded, that with the disguise and the engagement ring, you'd keep your distance—and because of his offer, I'd keep mine."

"Ah, yes. The offer." A cynical note colored his words. "A business of your own, wasn't it?"

"Yes," she confirmed. "When we met during the young-entrepreneur's contest, Dom realized I was desperate to open my own store and offered a deal. If I'd work for you for one year—keep our relationship strictly professional, no personal involvement—he'd finance Baby Dream Toys."

"Desperate?" He seized on the word, his eyes narrowing. "Why were you so desperate to start your own business?"

The question hung between them. "Because of my mother," she said at last.

He stilled, watching her closely. "Your mother?"

Grace bowed her head. "We were going to start the business together. We dreamed about it, planned it. She used to make the most beautiful stuffed animals. She'd call them her 'baby dreams.' That's where the name for the store came from."

"What happened, *cara?*" he asked gently.

"She died right before the contest." Grace's voice broke and she buried her hands in her face. "I wanted to open the store so much, to name it in her honor. It was wrong to deceive you, I know that. But at the time...all I could think of..." She shook her head, fighting for control.

"Why didn't you tell me?" he demanded. "When all the other deceptions were uncovered, why didn't you come clean? Didn't you think I'd understand?"

She crumpled his handkerchief in her fist. "You had all these wonderful, generous excuses for why I'd deceived you. But they weren't true. I knew when you found out my motivation was greed, you'd hate me. I'm sorry," she said, choking on the words.

He groaned, the sound low and rough. "*Cara,* don't. Don't cry. Of course I don't hate you." Crossing to her side, he swept her into his arms. Gently, he pushed her hair from her face and forced her to look at him. "Dad was right about one thing. If it hadn't been for that damned engagement ring, I wouldn't have been able to keep my hands off you."

He kissed her with an urgency she couldn't mistake, sweeping her into a firestorm of desperate need. She didn't resist. The thought never entered her mind. She loved Luc and she wanted him. If all he could give her were these few minutes, she'd seize them with both hands. "Luc, please..." she whispered.

He studied her expression intently. "Are you sure?" he asked. At her nod, he eased back and dropped his suit jacket to the floor. Next came his tie. Yanking the knot loose, he stripped off the red silk and tossed it to one side. It ribboned through the air, catching on a lampshade.

Eager to help, Grace applied herself to the buttons of his shirt, wanting to feel the hair-roughened skin beneath her fingers. "You never told me why you came back this morning," she said, dropping a string of kisses along his jaw. A minute later the shirt winged through the air, joining his jacket on the floor.

"Distracted. Forgot my damned briefcase."

He unfastened his belt and whipped it out of the loops. At the harsh sound of his zipper, Grace froze. She stared at Luc, seeing the passion that marked his high-boned face. His breathing was fast and irregular, his chest rising and falling as if he'd just run a marathon. Sensing her hesitation, he didn't touch her, simply waited, giving her the opportunity to retreat.

Never had she thought to find herself in such a position, where she'd feel such an urgent need for a man, be filled with such an all-consuming love, be so ready to forsake the teachings of a lifetime. And yet that was precisely what she intended to do. All doubts gone, she reached out and stroked the taut, muscular ridges of his chest, exploring at will from shoulder to abdomen. As her hand drifted lower, she hesitated, reluctant to traverse into uncharted territory.

"Your turn," he muttered, grasping the bottom of her sweater and pulling it over her head.

She emerged breathless and flustered. But the minute she looked at Luc, the minute she saw the intense yearning flare to life in his golden eyes, all doubt vanished. His hands slipped beneath the straps of her bra and he slid the narrow bands from her shoulders. When he released the hooks, the scrap of lace joined his tie on the lampshade.

For a long time they stood without touching, absorbed in a visual examination. Then Luc reached out and gently cupped her breasts and Grace's knees buckled. He caught her in his arms and kissed her—fast, hot, desperate kisses. Shedding his trousers, he peeled off her stretch pants with a speed that left her gasping.

"Maybe we should go to the bedroom," Grace suggested, tumbling back into his arms.

"The bedroom. Right." He toppled her onto the couch and followed her down. "Too far."

His mouth closed over hers again and his hands began a thorough, intimate exploration, each delicious caress driving her closer and closer to some sweet crisis, the intense pleasure almost painful.

"Luc," she said with a gasp, squeezing her eyes closed. "I can't take much more."

"Grace?"

Luc's voice seemed to float to her from a long distance. "What, Luc?"

He nuzzled her cheek. "I didn't say anything."

"I thought you said Grace."

"Only before meals."

"I'm too hungry to eat," she muttered, winding her arms around his waist and pressing her mouth to the strong line of his neck.

"Grace?"

She frowned, slowly opening her eyes. "What?"

Luc nibbled her lips. "What?"

"I mean, what do you want?"

He chuckled, the sound low and intimate. "You know what I want."

"No. I mean, why did you call my name?"

He pulled back slightly. "I told you. I didn't."

"Grace?"

They both stiffened, staring at each other in dawning horror. "Get off me, quick!" she whispered urgently, shoving at his chest.

Luc didn't move. "What—"

"Grace!" An appalled masculine voice spoke from the doorway to the living room.

"Oh, criminey!" No longer trying to escape, she buried her head in Luc's chest, attempting to disappear behind his broad shoulders.

Luc glanced down at her, then over his shoulder at the man and woman hovering just inside the living room. "Who the hell are you?" he demanded. "And what are you doing in my apartment?"

"Dear Lord!" The man continued to stare in shock. "I'm ... I'm Reverend—"

"I'm Miss Caruthers with child protective services," the woman interrupted, pushing past the reverend and stepping boldly forward. She brandished her clipboard like a sword. "I'm your case manager."

"No. You're not," Luc contradicted. "Miss Carstairs is our case manager."

"Not anymore. I've taken over. Her report was so strange—closets and laundry baskets and elopements and so forth—"

"Elopements?" the minister cut in. "Did you say elopements?"

Miss Caruthers nodded emphatically. "Elopements. Poor Miss Carstairs has made such a muddle of everything, they've taken her off the case." She pointed an accusing finger in Luc's direction. "And it's all your fault."

Luc glanced first at Grace, then back at the intruders. "Turn around," he snapped. "And no peeking."

Hesitantly, they complied and Luc yanked Grace to her feet. Scooping a handful of clothes off the carpet, he tossed a pair of slacks in her direction and pulled on his shirt. Not wasting a single second, she thrust her foot into the pant legs.

"You want to tell me how you got in here?" Luc demanded.

"The door was open," the reverend replied, in an apologetic voice. His head swiveled toward the clothes-strewn lamp and quickly jerked away again. "Would you mind telling me what elopement this woman is talking about? And what baby?"

Grace grabbed Luc's arm, as if to physically restrain him. "Don't say it . . ." she whimpered—to no avail.

"My elopement," Luc announced, snagging her bra off the lampshade and tossing it to her. "And Grace's elopement."

"You're *married?*" the reverend gasped, spinning around. His eyes practically popped out of his head and he whirled away again. "Oh, good heavens."

"Yes, we're married," Luc confirmed.

"No, no!" Grace denied, dressing with a speed she'd never before attempted. "You don't understand. Just give me a minute to explain!"

Miss Caruthers began scribbling madly and Toni, fed up with being neglected, began to cry. Grace gave serious consideration to crying, as well.

The minister's gaze seemed drawn to Toni like a magnet. "You have a *baby?*" he whispered in disbelief.

"No!" Grace shouted.

"Maybe!" Luc shouted louder. "It depends on who you are." He looked at Grace. "Where's Stefano's scorecard? I'm getting confused. Which story do we tell the minister?"

"There isn't a minister on our damned scorecard!" she practically shrieked.

"*Grace!*" the minister exclaimed, clearly shocked.

She shut her eyes. "I'm...I'm sorry." Peeking at Luc, she said, "Did I ever mention that my father is a Methodist minister?"

"No," he replied dryly. "I don't believe you did. Let me guess. This is him, right?"

"Bingo."

"I should warn you that if you aren't married, there will be dire repercussions," Miss Caruthers announced.

"May we turn around now?" Reverend Barnes requested.

"Sure. Why not," Luc agreed. He glanced at Grace. "Your sweater's on backward."

She folded her arms across her chest. "It's a new fashion statement. It's called 'caught in the act.'"

"You two," Miss Caruthers informed them, "are in deep trouble. I can guarantee there will be serious consequences if we discover you've been lying to us. Now are you or are you not married?"

Luc sighed, then forced a smile to his lips. "Now, Miss Caruthers," he began.

The social worker stumbled backward. "Get away from me, you...you...devil!" She looked at Grace. "This is what happened to Miss Carstairs, isn't it? We knew something was wrong when she let her hair down and started to wear makeup."

Grace touched her own loose curls self-consciously. "Yes, he seems to have that effect on women."

Miss Carstairs drew herself up. "Well, not me! He's not going to use his charms on me." She peered at Luc hopefully. "You weren't going to try your charms, were you?"

Reluctantly, Luc shook his head. "No. I guess not. I believe my charming days are over."

The social worker struggled to hide her disappointment. "We'll see what Mrs. Cuthbert has to say about all this. She's my superior. And I guarantee she won't be pleased!" Spinning around, she scurried from the room. A minute later, the front door slammed.

With deep dread, Grace glanced at her father. "I bet you're wondering what's going on," she said with a hesitant smile.

CHAPTER TEN

The Great Lie
Day 346 continues to darken—but all is not lost...

"I THINK WHAT'S GOING on here is painfully obvious," Reverend Barnes said, with more than a touch of irony.

"Yes...well..." Grace could feel the bright color returning to her cheeks and she scrambled for something innocuous to say. Something to help ease them into the coming conversation—or confrontation. "Gee, Dad. Your being here sure is a surprise."

"For both of us. I did try and call."

She stirred uncomfortably. "We kept missing each other."

"Yes, we did. Now I see why." He glanced around the room and Grace knew he'd misinterpreted the reason her possessions were so liberally scattered about. "You haven't been at your apartment recently, have you?"

"No," she replied, deciding a lengthy explanation wouldn't help the situation any. "How did you know I was here?"

"When I couldn't reach you at home, I stopped by your office. A very helpful security guard gave me this address, once I'd convinced him I was your father."

"Edward," Grace said with a sigh.

"I believe that was his name. Now. I think introductions are in order, don't you?" He looked pointedly at Luc, who stepped forward.

"Luc Salvatore, Reverend Barnes," he said, holding out his hand. "It's a pleasure to meet you."

"Under other circumstances, I might agree with you," the minister replied, shaking hands.

"I'm sorry about that," Luc said, though his gaze remained direct and unrepentant. "If the door had been shut properly, we would have all been saved some embarrassment."

Reverend Barnes chose not to comment. "You're Grace's employer, aren't you?" he asked instead.

"Yes, she's been with me for almost a year."

"And is she also your wife?"

Luc shook his head. "No. Not yet."

"You're certain? There seemed to be some doubt a few minutes ago."

"I'm positive."

"We're not married, Dad," Grace informed him quietly, though Luc's use of the word "yet" had thrown her. He couldn't possibly mean what she thought he meant by that, could he?

Her father glanced at her, a concerned frown lining his brow. "Considering what was going on here a few minutes ago, I'm not sure whether to be relieved or dismayed. What about the baby? Whose is it?"

"Toni is my niece," Luc said. "Grace is staying with me to help with baby-sitting duties. And for the record, our relationship has been regrettably innocent until today."

"Thank heavens," Reverend Barnes murmured, his relief palpable.

Before Grace could manage to insert a single word, Luc added, "You should also know that we applied for a marriage license last week."

Grace closed her eyes and groaned.

Reverend Barnes glanced from one to the other. "You're engaged?"

Grace glared at Luc, who merely smiled. Oh, he was clever, all right. He'd phrased his announcement very carefully and in such a way that she couldn't very well deny an engagement, much as she'd like to. What did she say now? That he hadn't actually proposed? That to the best of her recollection their engagement had come about through barked orders, demands and a certain amount of coercion. That she'd only agreed to marry Luc if push came to shove. If push came to shove? This wasn't a shove. It ranked more like a bulldozing.

"Yes," she muttered with ill-concealed resentment, "I agreed to marry him."

Her father's eyes narrowed. She knew that look. Many a wayward parishioner had seen it right before they'd broken down and confessed all their sins. "I'm beginning to realize there's a whole lot about this situation that I don't know," he said. "Nor am I sure I want to know. In fact, I'm positive I don't want to know." He studied the two of them for a brief instant, and Grace didn't doubt that he could read the guilt in their faces. At least, he'd be able to read her guilt. Luc managed to look slightly more enigmatic. "I'd like to make a suggestion if I may..." Reverend Barnes announced in a determined voice.

"You want me to make an honest women out of her, is that it?" Luc guessed.

"Yes, I do. Assuming you love my daughter." He clasped his hands together, the gesture betraying a certain level of nervousness. "Well, do you?"

After a brief hesitation, Luc nodded. "Yes, I love her."

Satisfied, Reverend Barnes relaxed and turned to Grace, his gaze less severe. "I know you're ready, willing and able to marry this man. You wouldn't have allowed ... er ... matters to progress so far, if you weren't in love with him. Am I right?"

What could she say to that? "Yes, Dad," she whispered.

"Then, it's settled. I suggest you two marry, and marry now. After what I just witnessed, I don't think that will be any too soon. I suspect it may actually be somewhat too late."

Luc didn't even try to hide his satisfaction. And Grace knew why he looked so pleased. By marrying quickly, they had a chance of keeping Toni. "You'll marry us right away?" he asked.

"If you have the license and the blood test, I have the authority. All you need is a witness." He looked at Grace. "A dress wouldn't go amiss, either."

"A white dress," Luc stated. "The one you have hanging in the back of the closet should do."

"Luc, may I speak with you in the bedroom, please?" she requested through gritted teeth. "Dad, you'll excuse us? I think we need to talk this over before leaping to any hasty decisions."

Her father nodded and Grace caught hold of Luc's hand, tugging him toward the guest bedroom. The door had barely closed behind them before her hurt and anger spilled out. "How dare you lie to my father! And ... and how dare you agree to marry me!"

"What the hell was I supposed to say? Tell him no, I don't want to marry your innocent, little girl—I just want to make mad, passionate love to her?"

"At least that would have been honest!"

"No, it wouldn't have been. I've changed my mind about an affair, Grace. I want to marry you."

She stared at him in disbelief. "You really will do anything to keep that baby."

He didn't deny it, not that she would have listened if he had. She turned away and wrapped her arms around her waist.

"Cara..." He came up behind, his hands dropping to her shoulders. "I know what I'm asking is unfair."

"Not to mention unreasonable, untenable and unethical."

"That, too. But would it be so bad?"

Jerking free of his grasp, she whirled around. "Be honest for once, Luc. Why are you doing this? Do you really want to marry me, or is this whole charade just to protect Toni?"

"Would you believe me if I said it was for you?"

She shook her head, tears filling her eyes. "No," she whispered. "How could I, after the extremes you've gone to, to keep Toni out of the hands of the authorities. You've told so many different stories, tried to con so many people, how do I know this isn't just one more lie to get what you want?"

A muscle leapt in his jaw, and his hands clenched at his sides. "You could try trusting me."

The words hung between them and Grace shut her eyes, wanting with all her heart to trust him, to believe he loved her, to allow herself to grasp with both hands the joyous possibility that they had a future together. But she'd just spent the past year clinging to a dream that would never materialize. She couldn't do that again. Because this time it wouldn't just be her hopes that were crushed, it would be her heart, as well. A tear escaped from the corner of her eye.

"Grace, please. Don't cry." He reached out to brush away her tear, but she evaded his touch. "Trust me. It'll all work out, I promise."

"You told me that once before and look where it got us." She searched his face with tear-washed eyes. "I told you I'd have an affair with you. We don't have to go to such extremes. You don't have to marry me." It was almost a plea.

"Yes," he contradicted, savagely. "I do. We will marry, Grace, even if I have to drag you to the altar."

"Because of Toni." It wasn't a question.

"If that's the only way to convince you to marry me, then, yes. Because of Toni."

So, now she had a choice. She could go through with the marriage or she could say no, and it would all be over. She could walk out the door, tell her father the truth and end her involvement with Luc. She never had to see him again if she didn't want to. Never see him again. Never be touched by him again. Never share another kiss, another laugh. Never be held in his arms or know true love again.

And Toni would be turned over to the authorities.

"Marry me, Grace," he urged. "I swear you won't regret it."

"I already regret it." She bowed her head, knowing she couldn't desert Toni, any more than she could explain the true situation to her father. Not when a single yes promised to give her what she wanted most in the world. "Okay, I'll marry you," she said, wiping her cheek with the back of her hand. "But it's going to be a marriage of convenience. I won't be your wife in anything but name. I won't live with you, I won't work for you and I won't share your bed. After a few months we'll have the marriage annulled.''

"You can't be serious!"

"I'm very serious," she flashed back. "I was wrong to agree to Dom's plan. I admit it. But no one was supposed to be hurt. Well, people did get hurt, and I won't make that mistake again. I'll do this one last thing for Toni's sake, and because I'm too much of a coward to tell my father the truth. But once Carina and Pietro return, it ends.''

"I'm not going to argue with you. But understand this . . ." He caught her by the shoulders, refusing to let go. "Today your father will marry us. And there won't be an annulment. After a few weeks or a month, once you've realized that an annulment is out of the question, we'll marry again in my church.''

She shook her head. "No!"

He ignored her. "I have a couple of errands to run. It won't take more than an hour. I'll call Alessandro and ask him to be our witness.''

"You're going to invite your family?"

"Just my brother. Dad already thinks we're married, and I don't think you want the rest of the rabble here.'' He lifted an eyebrow. "Do you?"

"I . . . I guess not."

"Get dressed, Grace. I won't be long.'' Then he swept her into his arms and kissed her, a gentle, lingering kiss that promised to make everything right again.

A kiss she didn't dare trust.

THE HOUR BEFORE her wedding passed with frightening speed. After checking to be sure her father didn't mind watching Toni, she prepared for the ceremony. Pinning her hair in a sophisticated pleat, she applied cosmetics and perfume with a light hand. Finally, she pulled the dress Luc had requested she wear from the closet.

It was a deceptively simple design, a mere slip of a dress, short-sleeved with a scooped neckline, made special by a matching bolero jacket. She lingered in front of the mirror, undecided whether or not to wear her pearl necklace and earrings with it.

A light knock sounded on the door. "Grace?" Luc called, stepping into the room. He stopped short at the sight of her. "Grace..." He whispered her name in a rough, deep voice. "You're beautiful, *mia amorata*."

She slowly turned from the mirror and faced him, struggling to hide her nervousness. He looked rather fine, himself, she conceded. He'd dressed in a black suit and snow white dress shirt. Gold cuff links glittered at his wrists and a gold tie tack anchored his red silk tie in place.

"Is Alessandro here?" she asked.

"Yes. It's almost time to start the ceremony." He approached, a jeweler's box in his hand. "But first I have something I'd like you to wear. It belonged to my mother, a gift to her from my father—also on their wedding day."

"Luc—"

He shook his head, holding out the long, narrow box. "You can't refuse. I won't allow it."

Reluctantly, she took the gift and opened it. She gasped. A dainty opal choker lay on a bed of black velvet. Vivid green and blue sparks mingled with almost every color in the rainbow and blazed outward from the center of each gem. "Fire opals?" she whispered.

"Yes. They were my mother's birthstone. Let me help you put them on." He lifted the choker from the box and slipped it around her neck. Then he bent down and pressed his lips to the sloping curve of her shoulder.

"Thank you," she said in a muffled voice. "You shouldn't have."

"I have something else." With a wicked grin, he reached in his pocket and pulled out a ruffled blue garter, dangling the scrap of silk and lace from his finger. "The opals are something old. This is both new and blue. Would you like me to put this on, as well?"

She couldn't help smiling. "I can manage, thanks."

"Which just leaves something borrowed." His hand dipped into his pocket once again. "I didn't know if these would suit your taste, so they're on loan until you decide whether or not you want them." In his palm nestled a pair of opal earrings, fire opals that perfectly matched the choker.

She shook her head, taking an unthinking step backward. "Oh, Luc... It's too much."

He shrugged. "Then, we can return them after the ceremony."

"Why are you doing this?" she asked anxiously, clasping her hands in front of her. "It isn't like this will be a real marriage."

She instantly realized she'd said the wrong thing. His expression closed over, growing cool and remote. "Put the earrings on," he requested in a clipped voice. "And the garter, too."

Not wanting to argue with him, after all the trouble he'd gone to, she accepted his gifts. Turning her back to him, she slipped on the garter, then the earrings. "I'm ready," she finally said, and faced him.

He took her hand in his. "Let's go."

She stared at their joined fingers. Was he afraid she'd cut and run if he didn't hang on to her? Given half the chance, she just might. She looked up at him, searching his face for a hint of his innermost thoughts. He returned her look, his golden eyes glittering with determination. But love? If he felt it, it wasn't apparent. Defeated, she dropped her gaze and walked with him into the living room.

Her father waited in front of the picture windows. When he saw her, an expression of pride and tenderness leapt to his face. He crossed to her side and Luc released her arm, stepping back.

"You look beautiful," Reverend Barnes murmured. Gathering her close, he whispered, "Are you certain, Grace? This is what you truly want?"

"Yes, Dad, it is," she responded quietly. "I want it with all my heart."

"Then I'm happy." He held her tight for an extra moment before setting her free.

Alessandro stood close by, Toni in his arms. As soon as Reverend Barnes returned to his stance by the windows, Alessandro took his place and dropped a kiss on Grace's cheek. "Welcome to the family," he said with a warm smile.

"Thank you."

Luc picked up a huge bouquet of pure white tea roses and handed them to her without a word. More moved than she could possibly express, she didn't resist when he cupped her elbow and drew her to stand in front of her father.

"Shall we begin?" Reverend Barnes asked, giving Grace a final searching look.

She nodded, careful not to allow her doubts to show. "I'm ready," she said.

"Very well, we'll begin." He settled his bifocals on the end of his nose. "Dearly beloved—"

The banging at the door drowned out his words. With a murmured excuse, Alessandro practically ran to throw it open. "What are you guys doing here?" he demanded in exaggerated surprise.

Rocco shoved past his brother. "You told us to haul tail over here or we'd live to regret it. What's going on?" Stef and Marc piled in after him.

"Yeah. What's going on?" they chorused.

The three stopped dead in the entrance to the living room, their mouths dropping open. Marc recovered first. "You're getting married?"

"Without inviting us?" Stef followed up.

Luc glared at Alessandro, his look promising retribution. "Yes, I'm getting married. If you want to witness it, stand next to Alessandro and be quiet."

"Give me Toni," Marc told Alessandro.

"No, I want to hold her," Rocco said.

"*I'm* holding her."

Luc thrust a hand through his hair. "I want you four to *shut up* or you're out of here!" He took a deep breath, then said, "Please continue, Reverend Barnes. I'm sorry for the interruption."

"Go ahead, Dad," Grace urged.

The minister glanced uncertainly at the four Salvatore brothers. "All right. Now, where was I? Oh, yes. Dearly beloved, we're gathered here today to join this man and woman in the state of holy matrimony, a state not to be entered into lightly." He focused a stern gaze on Luc and Grace, then his brow wrinkled in concern. "Why didn't you invite your brothers?"

Luc gritted his teeth. "Because they don't know how to behave in public. Proceed. Please."

Toni let out a loud wail. "Uh-oh," Alessandro interrupted. "Can we take five for a diaper change?"

"No!"

"Luc, be reasonable," Grace murmured. "Go ahead, Alessandro. Marc, mix up a bottle—just in case."

Luc turned on her. "You know full well that if you fill up the one end it comes out the other," he argued. "Marc, no bottle."

"Never mind, Marc," Grace said, exasperated. "*I'll* get the bottle."

Five minutes later, they gathered once again in the living room. Toni was cradled in Rocco's arms, cooing happily. Marc held the bottle, ready to insert it at the first squawk. Luc's face had settled into grim lines.

"Are we set?" he asked the room at large. "Any other comments, criticisms or concerns?" No one said a word. He nodded in satisfaction. "Then, we can begin."

Reverend Barnes cleared his throat. "Let's see... Dearly beloved—"

"We did that part already," Luc bit out. "We're currently in a state we shouldn't enter lightly."

"Amen to that," Reverend Barnes muttered.

Grace tightened her hold on Luc's arms. "Dad. *Please!*"

"Perhaps if we skipped to the crucial bits?" Luc suggested.

Reverend Barnes glanced uncertainly at Grace. "You don't object?"

"No, Dad. I don't."

"Very well. I must say, this is highly unusual, but if you both agree, I guess it's all right. Let's see... Oh, right. Do you, Luciano Salvatore, promise to love, honor and cherish this woman?"

"I do."

"And do you, Grace Barnes, promise to love, honor and obey—"

"Dad!"

"Don't interrupt your father, Grace."

She turned on Luc. "I will *not* promise to obey. It's archaic. If you get to cherish, so do I."

The doorbell rang—a long, strident, insistent ring. Luc muttered beneath his breath in Italian. Grace closed her eyes and sighed.

"I'll get it," Alessandro offered brightly.

A minute later, Dom hustled into the room. "What is going on?" he demanded. "Why have I not been told there is to be a wedding?" He regarded Luc and Grace with a hurt expression. "And why did you tell me you were married, when you were not?"

Luc sighed. "You know why."

Dom nodded grimly. "Because I would have thrown you out of the family if I had known you had a baby with Grace without benefit of a wedding ring. I still might."

"What?" Reverend Barnes stared at them in shock. His gaze slid to Toni, kicking and gurgling in Rocco's arms. "She's... she's your baby, Grace?"

"No!" She covered her face with her hands. "Dad, could you finish the ceremony? Please? I promise I'll explain everything then."

"I think you'd better explain everything now."

A loud, determined banging resounded through the apartment, and Stef ran to the door. Luc threw his hands into the air. "That's it. Who the hell's left to barge in here? Wait a minute. What about the police? They haven't shown up yet. In fact, they're the only ones who haven't."

"I came in their place," a tall, stunning brunette announced from the doorway, Stef at her side. "Cynthia Cuthbert, social services." She smiled at the horrified gathering, her gaze shifting slowly to Luc and Grace. "Hello, Luc. It's been a long time."

If the identity of their latest visitor came as a surprise, Luc didn't show it. "Not long enough," he said dryly. "Hello, Cynthia."

Marc elbowed Stef. "Cynthia? *The* Cynthia? The woman Luc couldn't charm?"

"*The* Cynthia," his twin confirmed gloomily.

The social worker glided across the room. "You must be Grace," she said, offering her hand. She lifted an eyebrow. "Am I interrupting something?"

"You know damned well you are!" Luc spoke up.

"If this little event has been staged for Antonia's benefit, I'm afraid you're too late. The jig is up." She planted her hands on her hips and fixed Luc with an annoyed glare. "I must say, I'm not at all happy with you. You've positively ruined my caseworkers. They're as giddy as schoolgirls. Am I the only woman in the world you haven't charmed the pants off of?"

"You're the second." He pointed at Grace. "And she's the third. Though it's not for want of trying, I might add."

"Don't feel bad," Cynthia told him sympathetically. "I'm sure you did your best." She glanced at her watch. "I'm afraid I have to get down to business now. I've come for Antonia."

Luc folded his arms across his chest and shook his head. "Not a chance." His brothers instantly formed a protective circle around the baby. "In one minute Grace and I will be married."

The social worker shrugged. "That won't matter. You lied, Luc. You told the department the two of you were already married. Ms. Cartwright warned you of the consequences, if you told any more lies, and you ignored her warning."

"Don't treat me like a child, Cynthia," Luc practically snarled. "We both know the department can make exceptions. I want you to make one now."

A smile of genuine amusement touched her perfect features. "You always did have a way with words. Tell me why I should make an exception for you. Because we were once...friends?"

"That's one reason. You also know my family. You know we'll take care of Toni, that she's safe with us."

"Um...excuse me," Reverend Barnes interrupted. "I'm very confused. Exactly whose baby is this, and why are you trying to take her away?"

"This I would like to know, too," Dom chimed in, folding his arms across his chest.

"She's *my* daughter," a voice spoke from behind them. "And no one's going to take her away. Not if I have anything to say about it."

Everyone turned. "Pietro!" Grace exclaimed in delight. "You're back."

"Back..." He held out Carina's hand. A diamond-encrusted wedding band decorated her third finger. "And married. Everyone, my wife, Carina Donati...Salvatore."

"Antonia is Pietro's?" Dom questioned in confusion. "*Per dio!* Am I told nothing anymore?"

Spying her daughter, Carina wrenched her hand free of Pietro's and darted across the room, snatching the baby from Rocco's arms. "Toni!" she cried, bursting into noisy sobs, Italian endearments falling as fast as her tears. She hugged her baby close, dropping frantic kisses on Toni's tuft of black hair. Pietro crossed to her side and peered down at his daughter, an expression of wonder dawning on his face.

"She's beautiful," he whispered, reaching out a tentative finger to touch a round, pink cheek. "Everything was so hectic before I didn't really notice." He looked up and grinned. "I have a daughter," he announced in a proud voice.

It took close to an hour to straighten everything out. To Grace's secret amusement, Pietro proved to be the one Salvatore capable of charming the uncharmable Cynthia. By the time she left, he'd managed to straighten out most of their problems and had set up an appointment to settle any final questions.

Grace stood quietly by her father, grateful for the supportive arm he'd wrapped around her. She watched the happy reunion with a calm facade she hoped concealed her inner turmoil. *Luc didn't need to marry her now.* And though the knowledge came as a relief, it also caused the most agonizing pain. But that pain was nothing, compared to what it would have been if they'd gone through with the wedding and the subsequent divorce.

It was time to face facts. Their marriage wouldn't have worked, not when Luc didn't love her. And no matter what he said, he didn't love her. Not enough, anyway. If she left now, she could leave with some dignity. A few minutes longer and she'd break down. She glanced up at her father. "I guess there's no more reason for the wedding," she told him quietly.

He covered her hand with his. "I'm sorry, Grace."

She blinked back tears. Obviously, he understood far more than she'd realized. Was her love for Luc so apparent? "Let's go, Dad."

"You're not going anywhere." Luc moved to stand in front of her, blocking her escape.

"Luc, don't," she pleaded. "Toni is safe now. You don't have to sacrifice yourself. There's no point."

"You're right. There is no point. Except this." He took her hand in his. "I want to marry you, *cara mia*. For real. Now. And it won't be a marriage of convenience. I love you, Grace. I want a forever kind of marriage with you, the kind with vows to love, honor and cherish...."

"Not obey?" she asked in a shaken voice.

He nodded in satisfaction. "Fine. And obey."

"Actually," Reverend Barnes interrupted, "I was planning to add just one more vow to all that. Love, honor, cherish and never tell another lie. Seems more appropriate that way, don't you think?"

"Done," Luc agreed. "Grace?"

She didn't dare believe. "Why, Luc? Yesterday you wanted an affair. It wasn't until Miss Caruthers found out we weren't married that you changed your mind."

He shook his head, his golden eyes dark and stormy. "Something else happened."

"What?"

"Your father walked in." He cupped her face in his hands, speaking softly, for her ears alone. "Making love to you was beautiful beyond compare. When he walked in the door, it became sordid. I could see it in your face. You were ashamed. And I realized I'd turned something beautiful, something you should remember with joy for the rest of your life, into something shabby. In that moment, I realized I didn't want an affair with you. Affairs end. And I don't want what we have to end. I don't want you just for my lover. I want you for my wife. I want a forever with you."

Tears shimmered in her eyes. "I love you, Luc."

"Bellissima mia," he murmured. "Haven't I told you how much I love you? You're the only woman I see any-

more. You've made me blind to all others. Awake or asleep, I see only your face, hear only your voice. The air I breathe is filled with your scent." He held out his hand. "Will you marry me?"

"Try and stop me," she said with a huge smile, and slipped her fingers in his.

Luc turned to Reverend Barnes. "From the top, Reverend. And this time... don't skip a single word."

And he didn't.

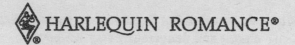

HARLEQUIN ROMANCE®

brings you

Harlequin Romance wishes you a **Merry Christmas...**
with two special Kids & Kisses stories!

In December, watch for *The Santa Sleuth*
by Heather Allison and *The Nutcracker Prince*
by Rebecca Winters.

Romances that celebrate love, families, children—
and Christmas!

The Santa Sleuth by Heather Allison
Virginia McEnery, age six, is the official "Santa sleuth"
on one of Houston's TV newscasts. Her job is to research
shopping mall Santas. And she whispers her Christmas
wish to every one of them. A *mommy*. Even though her
dad, Kirk, doesn't know it yet, she's already made her
choice—TV news producer Amanda Donnelly.

The Nutcracker Prince by Rebecca Winters
Anna Roberts, age six, wants a *daddy* for Christmas. Her
own daddy. Anna's sure he looks just like the handsome
Nutcracker Prince in her mommy's beautiful book. And
she's right! Because shortly before Christmas, her daddy
appears. His name is Konstantin and he's come here from
Russia. And he wants to marry Meg, her mom....

Available wherever Harlequin books are sold. KIDS7

Where do you find hot Texas nights, smooth Texas charm and dangerously sexy cowboys?

Crystal Creek reverberates with the exciting rhythm of Texas. Each story features the rugged individuals who live and love in the Lone Star state.

"...Crystal Creek wonderfully evokes the hot days and steamy nights of a small Texas community...impossible to put down until the last page is turned."
—*Romantic Times*

"...a series that should hook any romance reader. Outstanding."
—*Rendezvous*

"Altogether, it couldn't be better." —*Rendezvous*

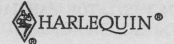

VOWS
Margaret Moore

Legend has it that couples who marry in the Eternity chapel are destined for happiness. Yet the couple who started it all almost never made it to the altar!

It all began in Eternity, Massachusetts, 1855.... Bronwyn Davies started life afresh in America and found refuge with William Powell. But beneath William's respectability was a secret that, once uncovered, could keep Bronwyn bound to him forever.

Don't miss **VOWS,** the exciting prequel to Harlequin's cross-line series, **WEDDINGS, INC.,** available in December from Harlequin Historicals. And look for the next **WEDDINGS, INC.** book, *Bronwyn's Story,* by Marisa Carroll (Harlequin Superromance #635), coming in March 1995.

WED7

1994 MISTLETOE MARRIAGES
HISTORICAL CHRISTMAS STORIES

With a twinkle of lights and a flurry of snowflakes, Harlequin Historicals presents *Mistletoe Marriages*, a collection of four of the most magical stories by your favorite historical authors. The perfect way to celebrate the season!

Brimming with romance and good cheer, these heartwarming stories will be available in November wherever Harlequin books are sold.

RENDEZVOUS by Elaine Barbieri
THE WOLF AND THE LAMB by Kathleen Eagle
CHRISTMAS IN THE VALLEY by Margaret Moore
KEEPING CHRISTMAS by Patricia Gardner Evans

Add a touch of romance to your holiday with
Mistletoe Marriages Christmas Stories!

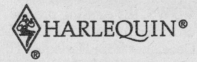

HARLEQUIN®

MMXS94

IT'S FREE! IT'S FUN! ENTER THE

☆ "Hooray for ☆
☆ Hollywood" ☆

SWEEPSTAKES!

We're giving away prizes to celebrate the screening of four new romance movies on CBS TV this fall! Look for the movies on four Sunday afternoons in October. And be sure to return your Official Entry Coupons to try for a fabulous **vacation in Hollywood!**

 If you're the Grand Prize winner we'll fly you and your companion to Los Angeles for a 7-day/6-night vacation you'll never forget!

 You'll stay at the luxurious Regent Beverly Wilshire Hotel,* a prime location for celebrity spotting!

 You'll have time to visit Universal Studios,* stroll the Hollywood Walk of Fame, check out celebrities' footprints at Mann's Chinese Theater, ride a trolley to see the homes of the stars, and more!

 The prize includes a rental car for 7 days and $1,000.00 pocket money!

Someone's going to win this fabulous prize, and it might just be you! Remember, the more times you enter, the better your chances of winning!

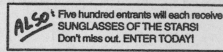

ALSO! Five hundred entrants will each receive SUNGLASSES OF THE STARS! Don't miss out. ENTER TODAY!

The proprietors of the trademark are not associated with this promotion.

CBSIBC

"HOORAY FOR HOLLYWOOD" SWEEPSTAKES

HERE'S HOW THE SWEEPSTAKES WORKS

OFFICIAL RULES — NO PURCHASE NECESSARY

To enter, complete an Official Entry Form or hand print on a 3" x 5" card the words "HOORAY FOR HOLLYWOOD", your name and address and mail your entry in the pre-addressed envelope (if provided) or to: "Hooray for Hollywood" Sweepstakes, P.O. Box 9076, Buffalo, NY 14269-9076 or "Hooray for Hollywood" Sweepstakes, P.O. Box 637, Fort Erie, Ontario L2A 5X3. Entries must be sent via First Class Mail and be received no later than 12/31/94. No liability is assumed for lost, late or misdirected mail.

Winners will be selected in random drawings to be conducted no later than January 31, 1995 from all eligible entries received.

Grand Prize: A 7-day/6-night trip for 2 to Los Angeles, CA including round trip air transportation from commercial airport nearest winner's residence, accommodations at the Regent Beverly Wilshire Hotel, free rental car, and $1,000 spending money. (Approximate prize value which will vary dependent upon winner's residence: $5,400.00 U.S.); 500 Second Prizes: A pair of "Hollywood Star" sunglasses (prize value: $9.95 U.S. each). Winner selection is under the supervision of D.L. Blair, Inc., an independent judging organization, whose decisions are final. Grand Prize travelers must sign and return a release of liability prior to traveling. Trip must be taken by 2/1/96 and is subject to airline schedules and accommodations availability.

Sweepstakes offer is open to residents of the U.S. (except Puerto Rico) and Canada who are 18 years of age or older, except employees and immediate family members of Harlequin Enterprises, Ltd., its affiliates, subsidiaries, and all agencies, entities or persons connected with the use, marketing or conduct of this sweepstakes. All federal, state, provincial, municipal and local laws apply. Offer void wherever prohibited by law. Taxes and/or duties are the sole responsibility of the winners. Any litigation within the province of Quebec respecting the conduct and awarding of prizes may be submitted to the Regie des loteries et courses du Quebec. All prizes will be awarded; winners will be notified by mail. No substitution of prizes are permitted. Odds of winning are dependent upon the number of eligible entries received.

Potential grand prize winner must sign and return an Affidavit of Eligibility within 30 days of notification. In the event of non-compliance within this time period, prize may be awarded to an alternate winner. Prize notification returned as undeliverable may result in the awarding of prize to an alternate winner. By acceptance of their prize, winners consent to use of their names, photographs, or likenesses for purpose of advertising, trade and promotion on behalf of Harlequin Enterprises, Ltd., without further compensation unless prohibited by law. A Canadian winner must correctly answer an arithmetical skill-testing question in order to be awarded the prize.

For a list of winners (available after 2/28/95), send a separate stamped, self-addressed envelope to: Hooray for Hollywood Sweepstakes 3252 Winners, P.O. Box 4200, Blair, NE 68009.

CBSRLS

OFFICIAL ENTRY COUPON

"Hooray for Hollywood"
SWEEPSTAKES!

Yes, I'd love to win the Grand Prize — a vacation in Hollywood — or one of 500 pairs of "sunglasses of the stars"! Please enter me in the sweepstakes!

This entry must be received by December 31, 1994.
Winners will be notified by January 31, 1995.

Name _____

Address _____ Apt. _____

City _____

State/Prov. _____ Zip/Postal Code _____

Daytime phone number _____
(area code)

Account # _____

Return entries with invoice in envelope provided. Each book in this shipment has two entry coupons — and the more coupons you enter, the better your chances of winning!

DIRCBS